The Darkness
AFTER

The Darkness AFTER

Scott B. Williams

Ulysses Press

Published in the United States by
ULYSSES PRESS
P.O. Box 3440
Berkeley, CA 94703
www.ulyssespress.com

ISBN 978-1-61243-184-0
Library of Congress Control Number 2013931789

Printed in Canada by Marquis Book Printing

10 9 8 7 6 5 4 3 2 1

Acquisitions Editor: Keith Riegert
Project Editor: Katherine Furman
Managing Editor: Claire Chun
Editor: Mary Hern
Proofreader: Elyce Berrigan-Dunlop
Cover design: what!design @ whatweb.com
Cover photographs: sunset © Hasloo Group Production Studio/
    shutterstock.com; archer © Mary Morgan/istockphoto.com
Arrow illustration: © Santi0103/shutterstock.com

For my dearest Michelle, always there for me, always believing I can do anything. With you, I can.

ACKNOWLEDGMENTS

I would like to thank acquisitions editor, Keith Riegert and the rest of the staff at Ulysses Press for taking a chance on my fiction last year with the publication of *The Pulse*, and for suggesting this parallel story. I would especially like to thank developmental editor, Katherine Furman, for patiently working with me to help make this story better than I envisioned and for providing exceedingly helpful feedback. I also want to thank my long-time friend, Mike Jones, game warden of Lawrence County, Mississippi, for providing insight into a difficult and dangerous job, and for showing me some of the equipment used by the Mississippi Department of Wildlife, Fisheries and Parks.

PROLOGUE

Mitch was annoyed at how hard it was to control the shaking in his arms as he held the bow at full draw and took careful aim. It was certainly not the sixty-pound draw weight of the longbow that made him unsteady—the physical part was easy after years of practice. He was so familiar with the bow that the mechanics of holding, aiming, and releasing were unconscious. He acted only on muscle memory until the arrow was on its way to its mark. Sometimes that mark was a stationary practice target, and as long as he didn't overthink it, he almost never missed. Other times the mark was a wary game animal that could at any instant hear a subtle sound, see the movement of the bow being drawn, or catch his scent before the arrow released. It was natural to have a touch of "buck fever" at such moments in a hunt, but with experience, he had long since overcome that nervous reaction. Every game species common to the area, from deer and wild hogs all the way down to rabbits and squirrels, had fallen to the arrows from that old-school wooden longbow. While he occasionally passed up a shot he deemed too marginal to take, he rarely missed a kill once he made the decision to let an arrow fly.

The shaking today was different altogether and much stronger than ordinary buck fever. His target was in easy range and out in the open, where no twig could deflect the flight of the arrow, but the stakes were higher than they had ever been. This time his arrow could save a life, but to do so, it would claim another—and not that of a game animal, but of a fellow human being. This was completely outside the range of experience of the sixteen-year-old archer, but then, so was most everything that had occurred this week.

The drama unfolding before him gave him no time to debate the moral implications of taking the shot. By whatever reason, maybe it was just chance, he happened to be in a position to impact a situation that had developed so fast it was a wonder there was even time to sneak close enough to get in range.

With a deep breath and slow exhalation, he regained control and willed his arms to stop trembling. The tip of the razor-sharp broadhead protruded just an inch beyond the back of the bent bow, ready to harness the power in those fibers of wood strained nearly to the breaking point. His breathing once again in control, Mitch corrected his aim and allowed the release of the string to happen automatically. There was the familiar snapping twang of the string, followed quickly by the dull smack of an arrow striking flesh.

He was shaking again as he reached for another arrow, but he placed it on the string and drew, breathing deep again to calm down. The element of surprise was gone, and the second target was running. There was no time to hesitate; he aimed for center of mass and let loose the arrow.

ONE

April held her breath as the Mustang's engine went dead a second time. It had already sputtered, lost power, and died just seconds ago, so she downshifted to second gear and popped the clutch. It started right back up and seemed to be fine, but she had barely gotten up enough speed to shift to third when it died again. This time it didn't restart, and after trying the clutch a couple more times, she steered for the shoulder of the road before the car lost all momentum and became another stationary object among the newer cars and trucks that were abandoned days ago. April turned the key again and again, spinning the engine with the starter to no effect until she finally gave up for fear of running down the battery.

Now what? What could possibly be wrong with this piece of junk now? The car had been running fine since she'd left New Orleans. It was far too old to be affected by whatever caused the power surge that fried the electronic engine controls in practically every vehicle built in the last thirty years or so, and despite cursing it, she knew she was lucky to have it. After getting it put back together and running, she was beginning to have hope she would make it all the way to Hattiesburg, until this.

She looked around before getting out of the car. The highway was a desolate scene of empty, parked vehicles with no sign of life or movement. Darkening clouds to the west promised approaching rain, and the heavy overcast sky that shut out the morning sun did nothing to improve the mood of this lonely place or lighten her spirits at the prospect of being stranded. Closer to the city, she had passed lots of people walking and even a few riding bicycles as she weaved in and out among the stalled cars and trucks blocking the lanes. But here, well out in the countryside, she was far from the crowds of stranded commuters and city dwellers, and pedestrians were few and far between.

She had made her way out of the city across the Twin Span Bridge over Lake Pontchartrain, staying on I-59 until she was beyond the outskirts of Slidell on the North Shore and across the state line into rural Mississippi. Along the Interstate, she had narrowly escaped people who had desperately tried to get in her car in places where she'd been forced to slow down to get through the obstacles on the road. One man had jumped on the Mustang from the rear and clung to the roof until she managed to fling him off with a sudden swerve. She knew that many of the people she passed along the way would likely do her no harm, but it was far too risky to take a chance. If she lost the car, she would be in the same situation they were in. Once she had made it over the bridge, she decided it was best to avoid as many of the walking refugees as possible, so she got off the Interstate and took a lesser-used highway that ran more or less parallel to that main artery out of the city.

This smaller, two-lane highway ran through a few towns and communities, but in between the landscape was mostly uninhabited swamps and woods. Where the Mustang had rolled to a stop, she saw one isolated house set back among a grove of pine trees west of the road, and on the other side behind a narrow buffer of trees were railroad tracks that ran parallel to the highway about a hundred feet away. Looking closer, she could see a wisp of smoke coming from behind the house— something she had seen at many of the other houses along the way. People were building fires to cook and heat water by day, and they kept them going at night for the comforting light. It was insane how everything had changed so fast, how modern life had ground to a halt in an instant, and people were trying to adapt any way they could. In just four days, most people were already reduced to near primitive conditions, camping beside their homes or in their vehicles.

April got out of the car and walked around to the front of the hood. It didn't make sense that it would go dead now when it was running fine so far. From the way it sputtered and stopped, her best guess was that it was simply out of gas. With a non-working fuel gauge, she had no way of knowing how much was in the tank when she'd left, and getting more in New Orleans was out of the question. David had spent more time working on it than driving it the entire time she'd known him, and with the latest carburetor problem, it was likely the tank had been well under half full while it had been parked in the alley beside their apartment for the past two weeks.

Money had been a struggle for them as long as they'd been together, and the old Ford had often been a source of resentment when April suggested that David should give it up for something more practical. He could barely keep the engine running, much less afford to fix all the nonessentials like the stereo, air conditioner, and gas gauge. The irony was that now his forty-something-year-old car was among the few that even had a chance of running, while her late-nineties Honda was practically worthless.

April pulled the latch and raised the heavy hood, it's rusty hinges squeaking loudly in the silence that hung over the deserted highway. She could hear the ticking sound of hot metal from the engine as she removed the wing nut holding the breather cover to check the carburetor. She sniffed for gas fumes but didn't smell any. The car was almost certainly out of gas and she had to get more, but how? She screwed the breather cover back on and slammed the hood in frustration.

All these stranded cars around her probably had fuel in their tanks, but how would she get it out? There had to be a way to siphon or drain some, but she didn't even have a container to pour it in to refill her tank even if she could figure out how to get some out. She looked in the direction of the lone house across the road, wondering if she could get some help from the people there. She was almost afraid to go over and ask, but just as she looked that way, she saw that she wouldn't have to.

Three men had suddenly appeared from around back and it was clear they had seen her. They were already striding across the lawn in her direction at a brisk pace. April stood by the car and waited. As they got closer, she began to wish they had *not* seen her. She had been around a lot of rough people in the various places she'd lived, and she was usually able to stay cool in such situations, but the looks of these three didn't inspire trust, nor did they look like they belonged at a rural house this far out of the city.

Just from the way they walked she could tell they had an attitude that didn't match the fear and confusion of most people she'd encountered since the lights went out. These three had the look of predators zeroing in on their next meal, but April knew better than to show fear and give them even more confidence. She stood her ground as they stepped up to the shoulder of the road from the grass. Now that they were just a few yards away, she could see that two of them were barely older than her—maybe just out of their teens but likely not over twenty-one or twenty-two. The one leading the way, though, looked like he could be forty or older. They all had the hard, tanned look of men who worked construction or some other kind of outdoor labor, but the leader, with his scarred face and tattoos of skulls and Rebel flags all over his arms, looked like someone who enjoyed fighting for his after-work recreation. He was the first to speak:

"Da-aaammn! What have we got here? Is that what I think it is? Is that a genuine 1969 Mustang Fastback?" The older man whistled as he took in the car. Clearly it was the kind of ride that had turned him on even before the blackout—before old relics like this were the only cars that would still run. "I told y'all it was a Ford V-8.

I could hear it coming a mile away," he said, glancing over his shoulder at his companions.

"That's all right," one of the younger men agreed, but his gaze had passed over the antique car and was fixed on April. He took her in from head to toe, not caring at all that his appraisal of her body was obvious. The third one was staring, too. It was like they hadn't seen a female in a long time, even though the blackout had just happened earlier that week.

The older one turned his attention from the car back to April. "Where'd a teenaged girl barely old enough to drive get a car like this? Your daddy buy it for you, sweetheart?" He grinned as he walked to the driver's side of the car and opened the door and slid behind the wheel. April was still standing in front of the car by the hood.

"It's my fiancé's car. Look, I think it's just out of gas. It was running fine until now, but the gas gauge doesn't work, so I didn't know how much I had until it ran out. I was going to walk up to your house over there and see if someone could help me. If you don't have gas, there's probably some in these other cars. I just need to get a few gallons so I can get to Hattiesburg."

"What's your hurry to go up there? If this Mustang belongs to your fiancé, then where the hell is he? Don't he know it's dangerous for a pretty girl like you to be driving around out here all alone? Ain't many cars that'll run at all after what happened, and there's a lot of people that would like to have a car like this about right now. Besides, you fill up with gas here, you'll just run out again somewhere else. Don't you know the situation is the same everywhere? It ain't gonna be no different in Hattiesburg."

April was about to explain the real reason she had to get to Hattiesburg, but then she thought better of it. These men were not likely to be sympathetic to her situation, and the best she could hope for was that they would leave her alone and give her a chance to figure out how to get more gas herself. But she already knew that wasn't going to happen. The older man seemed to have taken possession of David's Mustang as if it were his own. He pumped the accelerator and turned the ignition key, grinding the starter as April had done, with the same result.

"Yep, I think you're sittin' on empty all right. But that ain't nothin' to worry about. Like you said, we can get some gas out of one of these cars. But there ain't no hurry, 'cause time don't mean nothin' no more anyway. You oughta hang around and party with us for a while. You might forget all about that fiancé of yours that let you set out on the road like this by yourself without any gas. What's your name anyway, sweetheart? I'm Reggie, and that's my nephew, T.J.," the man said, nodding at the one who had stared at her first. "And that's his buddy, Danny," he indicated the other man, who had not yet spoken. "They ain't much older than you, and I'll bet they'd be glad to have a girl around to talk to."

"Hey, T.J., why don't y'all show her over to the house while I see if I can get some gas in this car and get it off the road?"

April said nothing, but glanced over her shoulders as the man was talking, trying not to be obvious, but looking at her options for an escape route. The situation did not look good. Even if she could outrun them, which she doubted, if she lost the car, her chances of getting to Hattiesburg would be slim. It would take days to walk there, even from here, and that was assuming she had plenty to eat and the strength to do it. She was determined not to give up the car without a fight.

The older man was still sitting in the driver's seat of the Mustang, looking at the details, running his hand over the upholstery. "You just don't know how much I always wanted one of these back when I was a kid your age. Say, where'd you learn to drive a stick anyway? I didn't think anybody under thirty even knew what one was these days."

"Girls like her know a lot more'n you give 'em credit for, Uncle Reggie," the one he'd called T.J. said. "I'll bet that ain't all she's good at."

April backed up against the hood of the car as T.J. stepped toward her, keeping her right hand behind her, out of his sight as she waited for him to close the distance. If she was going to do anything to stop them, she had to act now and act decisively before T.J. or all three got their hands on her. Their intentions were clear, and if they were this bold right out here on the open road in the broad daylight, they obviously knew there was no one else around to intervene. If they got her inside the house, all bets were off and she wouldn't have a chance. She was determined to fight for all she was worth to make sure that didn't happen. The rules had changed, and April knew that if she was going to survive, she couldn't play by the old ones.

She waited until T.J. grabbed her by the left upper arm and pulled her in close to him. He reached for her hair with his other hand, so sure of his ability to drag her to the house with little resistance that he was oblivious of her right hand, with which she was reaching for something in the back pocket of her jeans. April felt the familiar textured grip of the Spyderco folding knife she kept there, and when her fingers closed around it, it was out of her pocket in an instant; the four-inch blade snapped to the open position with a flick of her thumb. T.J. was so preoccupied with thinking about what he was going to do to her that he didn't realize what was happening until it was too late.

April twisted her body beneath him and brought her knife hand up between his arms and straight to his unprotected throat, where the short blade could do the most damage with the least amount of effort. When she felt the serrated edge meet soft flesh, she sliced as hard and deep as she could, almost losing her grip with the force of the effort. The effect was immediate. The man staggered back and clutched at his wound, trying to stem the fountain of blood spurting between his fingers while his brain was still able to process the shock of what had just happened. April quickly stepped back and around to the passenger's side of the car, putting more distance between herself and his companion, who was momentarily paralyzed with disbelief. But then the other one screamed "T.J.!" as he watched his friend collapse to the ground and then turned to her with fury in his eyes.

"STAY BACK!" April shouted, holding the bloody knife in front of her as she backed toward the rear of the car to gain more distance before he could rush her. "I'll cut you, too, if you don't leave me alone!" He hesitated for a moment, unsure what to do, as he was unarmed and clearly shocked by what she'd done to his friend, but then she heard the car door slam as the older man got out.

"Get her, Danny! Don't let her get away!"

April turned and ran as the younger man rushed her. She had enough of a head start to sprint past the rear of the car before he could get around to the passenger's side, but the older man was right behind her, chasing her down the highway. He was much faster than she had imagined. He caught up with her before she had covered thirty paces, and grabbed her by the hair as he overtook her. She tried to slash at him with the knife, but he yanked her off balance before she could connect, causing her to drop her weapon as she fell hard onto the gravel shoulder. She rolled and twisted to get out of his reach. Her fingers closed around a handful of the small rocks that she was determined to hurl in his face as a last resort. She saw him bend over to pick up the knife she'd dropped, and it was clear that he intended to do to her exactly what she had done to T.J. But then something really strange happened . . .

The man suddenly fell for no apparent reason, collapsing to the roadway beside her when his knees buckled beneath him. She couldn't understand what caused him to fall, but after he was down, she saw blood pooling on the pavement beneath his body. The other attacker, who had caught up and stopped to watch as she was grabbed and thrown to the ground, turned to run back in the direction of the car, terrified by something he'd seen. But before he could reach the passenger side door, he too collapsed. It made no sense to April, who hadn't heard a thing, but then she saw something bright standing out in stark contrast to the black of the second one's T-shirt where he was thrashing facedown by the car. The strange object was just to one side of his spine, where the kidney would be. Blood was welling up around it and spilling onto the road just as it was around the older man who had fallen. It was then that April recognized the bright object for what it was: the tail end of an arrow, with a fletching of brilliant yellow feathers.

TWO

April scrambled to grab her knife and then quickly got to her feet. Her hands were scraped from the hard fall onto the gravel, but she put the pain out of her mind as she looked around for whoever had taken out her attackers with, of all things, arrows. When she looked back along the highway in the direction toward New Orleans, she saw a lone figure step up to the pavement from the high grass in the ditch, holding what could only be a bow. The figure was dressed from head to toe in hunter's camouflage, and if not for his movement, it would have been impossible to spot him against the backdrop of bushes.

The archer was walking her way, and April's first impulse was to turn and run. But she knew if he wanted to shoot her, running wouldn't do any good. She told herself that if he wanted to kill her, he would have done it before revealing himself. She stood her ground, determined that if he did shoot her, it would not be in the back.

Her four-inch knife was little better than nothing against a weapon that could kill from afar, but the adrenaline from using it on the first attacker still coursed through her body. *Had she really cut a man's throat?* She had felt the resistance of flesh against the edge of the blade, and there had been a fountain of blood as he staggered back. *But was he really dead?* If he was, he was on the ground in front of the car and she couldn't see him from where she stood. She glanced at the other two and was sure that both of them were dead. The one hit in the back had thrashed for a few seconds but was now still.

As the archer approached, he raised one hand in a friendly wave and removed the floppy camouflaged hat that shadowed his face. She could see that he was smiling in a way that she took to be an attempt to reassure her. He called out to her, saying he would not hurt her. Although an arrow was on the string at the ready, he carried the bow loosely in one hand, down by his side in a non-threatening way. April could see a cluster of bright arrow feathers protruding over his shoulder.

She waved back and tried to return the smile, lowering her knife as she did but still keeping her grip white-knuckle tight as she waited for him to get closer. When he did, she was surprised to see that the bowman was not really a man at all, but a boy—clearly young enough to still be in high school. He was not what she expected, considering what he had just done, but she kept her guard up and said nothing until he spoke again:

"Are you okay? Are you hurt? I know you must be scared after what just happened, but you don't have to worry, I won't hurt you. I saw what was going on and it was pretty clear that you needed some help."

"I'm okay, and I'm not scared. This wasn't my fault," April said a little indignantly even though she was still trembling. She brushed the dirt off the knees of her jeans with one hand, still holding the knife in the other. Her left knee felt bruised from the fall. "I wasn't looking for trouble. I just ran out of gas and wanted to get some more so I could keep going. I didn't want anybody to die." April glanced in the direction of the house the men had come from. "They came out right after I got out of my car. I think they heard the motor and probably wanted to steal it."

"I'm sure they did, and then they saw you and thought they could do whatever they wanted because you were alone. They probably would have killed you." As he said this, he walked past her to the lifeless bodies of the two he had taken out with his arrows. He continued on to search in the grass beyond the shoulder of the road and bent to pick something up. April saw that it was another arrow, red with blood. It was the one that killed the older man, the one she had never heard or seen, that had passed completely through his neck and landed several yards beyond. The boy then walked to the front of the car to check the third man, the one she had sliced across the throat with her knife. She didn't want to see, so she stayed where she was.

"You sure gave that one a surprise. Where did you learn to handle a knife like that, anyway?"

"I used to practice with my dad, a long time ago. Is he . . . ?"

"Yes, he's quite dead."

April looked down at the knife in her hand, for the first time noticing the blood that covered the blade. She bent down and wiped it in the grass near the shoulder of the road, keeping her eyes on the archer as she did. "My dad was into martial arts. He grew up in Okinawa and studied both Shorin-ryu and Aikido. After that, he had been an instructor for years as a young man, and even after I was born, and he still kept up his training. He taught me a lot about both armed and unarmed self-defense, but just in an informal way. He said the knife was one of the easiest weapons to carry, and that I should always have one with me. He gave me my Spyderco and I have always kept it close, mainly because it reminds me of him. I've never needed it for anything but opening the mail until today."

"He sure taught you well judging by how you handled yourself. Look, you didn't do anything wrong. You did what you had to do, and no one would blame you, just like you don't blame me. I've never aimed my bow at another human being until today either, but I'm sure glad I had it. I'm Mitch, by the way."

"I'm April," she said. "I'm glad you showed up, Mitch. I guess you're right. I probably couldn't have stopped those other two, so if it hadn't been for you, I don't know . . . But where did you come from? I didn't see anyone else around here when I got out of the car."

"I was resting behind some roadside bushes about a half mile back, in the strip of woods between the highway and the railroad. I was trying to get some sleep after walking the tracks all night. I heard you drive by, and at first I thought I was dreaming. There just aren't many motors running since the blackout, you know. I jumped up and ran to edge of the highway in time to hear your car starting to cut out. I started walking this way because I wanted to see who it was that had a running car and if I could help get it going again. Mainly, I was hoping for a ride if it would still run. Before I got halfway here, I saw those guys come up onto the road and I slipped back into the ditch to stay out of sight as I came closer. Something about them just didn't seem right, and I saw that you were alone."

"I can't believe how you hit them like that and they never saw you, and neither did I. Where did you learn how to shoot a bow and arrow like that? You must be some kind of hunter or something."

"Yeah, I hunt. I grew up on six hundred acres of woods in Mississippi. I've been hunting all my life. I've been into the bow and arrow since I was old enough to shoot the toy kind with rubber-tipped arrows. I started hunting with real bows when I was about eight. I just like archery, and I've always preferred the bow and arrow to guns, but I sure wish I had my rifle, or at least a good handgun, with me now."

"You have your own guns? How old are you, anyway? You must still be in high school, right?"

"I am. I'm a junior this year, though. I just turned sixteen. You've got to still be in school yourself, right?"

"Ha, ha. No, I know I don't look it, but I'm eighteen. Everybody thinks I'm about fifteen, though, even after they see Kimberly."

"Kimberly?"

"My baby, my little girl. She's just over a year old."

"Wow, I never would have believed you had a kid of your own. Where is she, she's not in the car is she?"

"No, I wish. But if I had her with me, I wouldn't be out here on the road to begin with. As far as I know, she's still in Hattiesburg. At least I hope that's where she is. David, her daddy, well, his parents were keeping her overnight last weekend and I was supposed to go pick her up Monday morning, but I got called in to work, so he took my car and drove up there Monday night after he got off work. He was going to stay overnight and bring her back to New Orleans Tuesday morning, but then of course, whatever it was that happened and caused the power to go off and all the cars to quit working happened early that morning. I couldn't call him, and I'm sure that my car isn't running, so he couldn't bring her back home. I just hope he wasn't already out on the road with her when it happened."

"So the Mustang belongs to your husband?"

"Boyfriend. Well, fiancé, I suppose, though it's not official. We were supposed to be married by now, but that's another story."

"So your car must be a newer one?"

"Hardly new, but yeah, it's a '99 Honda Accord, so new enough that it won't run."

"Well, his Mustang sure is pretty sweet. There can't be anything under the hood of it that's high-tech enough to be affected if you got this far. What do you think is wrong with it?"

"I'm pretty sure it's just out of gas. It wasn't running at all when this blackout thing happened. That's why David took my car. He was having carburetor problems and had bought a rebuild kit for it. He went off and left the parts all over our kitchen table. I didn't do anything that first day but pace the floor. I kept hoping my phone would somehow come back on or David would just drive up and everything would be okay. By the next day, I heard people around my neighborhood talking about what could have happened. Everybody seemed to think it was some kind of electromagnetic pulse from the sun."

"I think that's probably it," Mitch said. "Most likely it was caused by a solar flare, but nobody seems to know for sure. There were some news stories last year, though, about how something like this *could* happen, but I don't think many people really believed it would."

"Well, some people were saying old vehicles weren't affected by it. Then I saw some running that second day. Not many, but every once and a while, I would hear an old car or truck going by on our street. I started thinking that since this Mustang was built in the '60s, it would probably run, too. I just had to get that carburetor back together and put it back on."

"You did that by yourself? That's pretty impressive!"

"I *had* to. I knew there was no other way to get to my baby. I had watched David take it off, so I knew how to put it back on. I worked on it all the next day. I was afraid to ask anyone for help, because I didn't trust them not to steal the car. It was kind of hidden in the alley beside our apartment, so hardly anyone in the neighborhood knew it was there. The hardest part was putting the carburetor back together with the rebuild kit. But the kit did come with instructions and a diagram, showing where all the gaskets and parts went. David left his tools, so I was able to do it. Honestly, I think I may have done it even faster than he could have," April laughed to herself and shook her head. "That's why I just left today instead of the day all this happened. I would have almost been there by now, if I hadn't run out of gas. I didn't know how much was in the tank. The gauge has never worked since he bought it."

"Wow, now I'm *really* impressed. You put that carburetor back together and got it running all by yourself, with no mechanical experience? That's amazing."

"You do what you've gotta do when you have a child," April said, "no matter how much you don't want to." She glanced at the knife she was still holding and then folded the blade back into the handle. She put it back into her pocket, starting to relax a bit for the first time since the three men approached her. She felt confident that Mitch wasn't a threat, but she still had a lot of questions. "You said you were walking all night; where were you going?"

"Home," Mitch said. "My family's land is about forty miles northeast of here. I was in New Orleans, too, when the solar flare hit."

"You've walked all this way? What were you doing in New Orleans dressed like that, and carrying a bow and arrows?"

"That's a good question, isn't it? Well, for one thing, I've just about always got my bow with me. I usually have my .357 Magnum revolver under the seat, too, at least if I'm driving my own truck. But like a fool, I didn't take the gun that day; I knew I'd be driving across state lines, and it would be just my luck some New Orleans cop would stop me and find it. Since I'm not twenty-one, I'm not legally old enough to have a handgun, but back home in Perry County, nobody cares.

"Anyway, I was in my dad's truck because I was taking him and my mom to the New Orleans airport to catch an early flight and my truck doesn't have a back seat. I put the bow and my camo stuff in there because I wasn't going back to school that day anyway, and I figured I could drop them off and get back to the woods early enough to do some wild hog hunting before my little sister got home from school.

"Of course my dad's truck, being a brand new Ford F-150, just shut down right in the middle of the street while I was sitting at a red light. It happened about an hour and a half after their flight was scheduled to leave, and I still don't know if they made it to Houston in time or not. I could hear an explosion from at least one plane crash in New Orleans from where the truck stopped."

"Oh my God! You must be worried to death about them then!"

"I *am* worried, but I feel like they probably got to Houston before it happened. Like most flights out of New Orleans, they had a connection there and it was supposed to be a flight time of just about an hour. Unless something delayed their plane taking off or landing, they would have had enough time to get back on the ground there. If they did, they're stuck in a bigger city than New Orleans, and I know it'll be dangerous, but at least they'll be alive. My dad would know what to do in any case, and I figured there was nothing I could do for them right now. There's really no way to find out if they're okay, but I have to get back to Mississippi and look out for my little sister. She was at a friend's house the night before all this happened, and I'm sure she stayed with them, but I'm still worried about her. I know she's got to be scared and worried about Mom and Dad, too. So I started walking out of the city, but

I figured it was safer to travel at night and stay out of sight in the daytime, even after I got way out there and was walking the railroad tracks. That's why I happened to be near here trying to rest when you drove by, and the loud exhaust on that old Mustang woke me up."

"I'm glad it's so noisy then. I didn't like listening to it when David had it running before, and I've been worried about it attracting too much attention, but I guess that can be a good thing once in a while."

Mitch nodded. "Look, it's going to be raining soon, and it looks like it might set in for days, judging by those clouds. We'd better get some gas in your tank and see if it will still start again. Since you're heading to Hattiesburg anyway, I wonder if I could bum a ride part of the way? Our land is not far off your route, and it would save me a couple more nights of walking."

"Absolutely," April said. "That's the least I could do. There's got to be gas in some of these abandoned cars and trucks, but I didn't have anything to get it out with. Do you have any ideas?"

THREE

Mitchell Henley still had moments when he hoped the new reality he found himself in was a dream he would surely wake from. Had he *really* just killed two men with his hunting bow? Did this young woman who looked more like she was fifteen than the eighteen years she claimed just cut a man's throat with a folding knife? It seemed impossible that the fabric of civilization could unravel in just a matter of days after the failure of technology, but everywhere he looked, it was happening. Mitch had practically grown up in the woods, and he much preferred to be outdoors than inside, but it was clear that almost everyone else was absolutely freaking out at the loss of their comforts, conveniences, and security.

He would have found it amusing if not for the suffering that it was causing those who had no chance of survival because they were too old or too young or too sick. Practically everyone, rich and poor alike, was stranded and isolated, facing the prospect of running out of food and medications and all the other essentials required to survive. All that was bad enough, without the added problem of having to fight off human predators like these three who saw the situation as a opportunity to take whatever they wanted from those they thought were weaker.

Mitch knew such men didn't turn this way overnight, and people like that probably would have done the same thing if they had the opportunity before the blackout. But in leaving the city of New Orleans, he had seen enough desperation to make it clear that even people who would never harm anyone in ordinary circumstances would soon be driven to drastic measures in order to survive. It was the inevitable outcome for any place that had a lot of people crammed together and nothing left to sustain them after the shelves of all the grocery stores were stripped.

Mitch didn't like towns, much less cities. He didn't like the noise, the traffic, and the houses all packed together in rows with barely any space between them. Growing up as he had, surrounded by almost six hundred acres of private land passed down from his grandfather to his father, living in such a crowded place was incomprehensible to him. There was no freedom to be found where there were so many other people and so many idiotic little rules you had to follow. That lack of free will was the main thing he hated about school, too; it was nothing but one rule after another, and along with structure and confinement, it amounted to the antithesis of everything he loved about the woods.

He endured it because he had to, but when he was in the classroom, he was always daydreaming about hunting or simply being out in nature, walking the trails or sitting under a tree listening to the silence. He knew that even the people in the rural county where he lived and went to school didn't share the same affinity he had for being outdoors. He had always been different that way. Not that he was alone in his interest for hunting, fishing, archery, and woodcraft—it was just that for him it was *everything*.

A few of his classmates who grew up on similar tracts of land in the country certainly hunted, but they looked at it as just another sport, something you do when it's in season, like playing football or baseball. Some of them were even quite good at it, but he didn't know of any who would be happy about having to hunt for all their food and live without electricity and running water. A lot of them and their families might be able to adapt and survive, though, depending on how long all of this lasted, but he didn't have much hope for the throngs he'd seen stuck in New Orleans and unable to get out. It would be the same in cities everywhere in the range of this pulse event, and that could be all of North America and even beyond, for all anyone knew.

If what he'd heard people in the city saying was true, and it really took weeks or months to rebuild all the systems that were destroyed, just how bad were things going to get in the meantime? It didn't bode well that so much violence had started just days after the collapse. After what happened here on this deserted stretch of highway, Mitch felt a renewed sense of urgency to get back to his little sister. He could protect her as long as they were on their own land, buffered from the madness by all those acres of woodlands and pastures.

Chancing upon April was fortunate for both of them—for her because she probably couldn't have defended herself against the other two enraged thugs after she killed the first one, and for him because she had a vehicle that could get him home a couple days sooner than if he had to walk the rest of the way. There was no time to waste getting it running again so they could start moving, and besides, he wanted to get away from the gruesome scene before someone else came along and started asking questions.

If she was right, and the car was simply out of gas, he was confident they could get more out of one of the nearby abandoned vehicles. He smiled when she asked if he had any suggestions on how to get some out.

"Yeah, I've got an idea how. I just need to walk over to that house and see if I can find a Mississippi Credit Card."

"A *credit card*? What good will a credit card do out here? Even if there were a gas station, it wouldn't work with the power out and the phone lines down. Everybody is saying plastic is worthless now."

"I'm not talking about the plastic kind. I'm talking about the *rubber* kind."

"What?"

Mitch just laughed. "Wait right here, I'll show you."

"I'm going, too. I don't want to be alone out here."

"Okay, but you stay behind me. I want to make sure no one else is watching us from inside that house. They probably would have run out here when everything started, but I'm not taking any chances."

"Fine by me," said April.

Mitch made his way across the yard with his bow in front of him, at the ready. He motioned to April to stay back as he approached the nearest window and looked in. He staggered back a step, almost losing his balance, then went around to the open back door to get a better look at what he'd seen from the window.

"DON'T COME ANY CLOSER, APRIL!"

"Is there someone there?"

"Just wait there, I'll be right back."

Mitch tried to put the grisly scene in the house out of his mind for a moment so he could turn his attention back to what he was looking for. He walked to the side of the house and motioned for April to follow, but at a wide berth. He pointed to spot near some bushes for her to hide while he continued on around back.

Just as he'd expected, coiled on a wire stand beside an outside water spigot was a garden hose. He whipped out his knife and sliced a four-foot section off the end, then he picked up an empty water bucket that was turned upside down nearby. "*This* is a Mississippi Credit Card," he said as he walked back to where she was waiting.

"Well, I knew you could siphon gas with a piece of hose, I just don't see why you call it a credit card."

"That's what my Grandpa used to say. Back in the Depression, when nobody could afford gas, they borrowed a little here and there with a piece of hose: a *Mississippi Credit Card*! It'll probably come in real handy now."

April forced a slight smile, then her face darkened, as if she could see something in his eyes. "What did you see in the house? There was no one there, right? Why did you want me to hide?"

"I can tell you that any remorse I may have felt for killing those two is forever gone now, and I can assure you that you did the right thing in killing the other one, too."

"What did they do?"

"There are two more bodies inside the house, April, right on the kitchen floor; an old man and an old woman, probably a married couple who lived here alone. Those three murdered them in cold blood." Mitch didn't wait for her reaction as he kept walking to her car. "Have you got any tools in the Mustang?"

"Yeah, I grabbed the wrenches and a few things David left at the apartment."

When she opened the trunk, Mitch searched around for a second and found a big screwdriver. "This will work." He took it, the hose, and bucket to a nearby GMC Yukon. "If this thing was even half full when the owner left it, it'll have more than enough gas in the tank to fill us up," he said.

The flimsy sheet metal fuel door was easy to pry open with the screwdriver, and soon he had the gas cap off and he inserted the hose into the fuel tank. He put his mouth over the open end and sucked on it to get the siphon started, dreading the inevitable mouthful of gas that was sure to follow. When it did, he quickly moved the end of the hose to the bucket, spitting and coughing to get rid of the taste and smell before it made him throw up.

"I hate siphoning gas!" he said. "I wish I had a cordless drill so we could just drill a hole in the bottom of the tank and drain it, but at least this way, if all this mess ever gets straightened out, whoever owns this truck won't have a ruined fuel tank."

"How long do you think it'll be before they get the power back on and fix everything?" April asked.

"I don't know. Who are *they* anyway? The power companies and the city and county officials, and the entire government for that matter are just as shut down as everybody else. How are they going to fix anything when *nothing* is working? Where are they going to come from, if this pulse thing really did affect the whole country?"

"We don't know that it did, do we?"

"No, but we don't know that it didn't, either. I haven't seen any kind of outside help coming around, have you?"

Mitch took the end of the hose out of the full bucket and handed it to April, instructing her to keep her thumb tightly over the end of it to maintain vacuum so they could get more without having to restart the siphon. He carried the bucket to the Mustang. He cut off the top of a cardboard box that was in the trunk and used it for a makeshift funnel. He stopped to look around for signs of anyone approaching before he went back to get more.

The highway was still deserted, much to his relief. The bucket only held two gallons, and he wanted to put at least five or six gallons in the car to be sure they had enough to get to the farm.

The rain had already started, just a light drizzle now, but he knew enough of these early spring weather systems to know that it would probably rain for the next two or three days. Conditions like that wouldn't make anything easier, but at least they wouldn't have to walk in it if the car started as he hoped it would. When he had poured two more buckets of fuel into the tank, April slid behind the wheel and turned the key. The starter spun but nothing else happened. She tried it again. Nothing.

April banged her hand on the wheel. "The last thing we want to do is run down the battery." She opened the hood and removed the breather cover again as she'd done when she checked it before the three men approached. "When I followed the instructions for putting the carburetor back together, there was something about having to prime it before the car would run. I used the starter fluid spray David had bought with the rebuild kit. Dammit! Why didn't I think to bring it with me?"

"Of course, that makes sense," Mitch said. "You ran it completely out of gas, and these old carbureted cars sometimes have to be primed to get the fuel flowing again. We don't need starter fluid; just a spoonful of gas will do the trick, I'll bet. There's enough left in the bottom of the bucket. Let's try that and see what happens."

They did, and when April got in and tried it again, the 302 V8 roared to life. She revved the engine to make sure it wasn't going to go dead again. Mitch put the breather cover back on and slammed the hood shut with a grin. "Let's get the hell out of here!"

FOUR

Mitch put his daypack and bow behind the two front seats of the Mustang, keeping the bow strung and ready for use with his quiver of arrows next to it, then slid into the passenger seat beside April. She shifted the car into reverse, backing up just enough to get around the body lying in front of the car, and then worked through the forward gears until she was in third. It wasn't safe to go faster than fifty miles per hour because she had to dodge so many stalled vehicles and obstacles.

The rain had picked up now, and Mitch was relieved to see that the old car's windshield wipers still worked. Mitch wouldn't have guessed she could drive a standard transmission so smoothly, but looking at her, he wouldn't have guessed she was old enough to have a child, either. If anything, she looked younger than him, but despite her innocent look, she had wielded that knife with skill and decisiveness he could hardly be-

—

lieve, especially in the face of such overwhelming odds. Knowing that she was a mother explained her fearlessness somewhat. She was not going to let anyone or anything stop her from getting back to her baby, even if that meant she had to cut someone's throat. It was a basic animal instinct that Mitch knew would come back to many people now—at least to those who were going to be survivors.

The man she'd killed deserved what he got. Mitch knew that all three of them did, especially after seeing the bodies of the old man and woman inside the house, apparently beaten to death. But even if those men hadn't murdered the couple, what they'd attempted to do to April was enough to justify her action and his, too. Any decent human beings would have tried to help a stranded young woman refill her car and get back on her way, but instead, they were clearly planning to take the car and do unspeakable things to her. He had not expected to have to use his hunting weapons against other people, but he could feel no remorse that he had done so in this case. These three wouldn't harm anyone ever again, but it was inevitable that more low-life predators like them would try to take advantage of the helpless. As long as this situation lasted, he could never again afford to be careless or unprepared.

April interrupted his thoughts when she asked about his journey on foot out of the city: "So, you just walked out of the middle of New Orleans, dressed like a deer hunter and carrying a bow and arrows?"

"Yeah, what else *could* I do? Right when it happened, I had taken an exit in Metairie to stop and get some breakfast before I got in the traffic heading across the bridge to Slidell. I was just sitting at a red light, waiting for it to turn green, when all of a sudden it just went completely out. At the same time, my dad's truck went dead. I was shocked—it was almost brand new. Then, I noticed all the cars and trucks around me weren't moving, either. People were getting out and opening their hoods, so I got out, too. Then, we all were asking each other questions, and we soon figured out that no one had a cell phone that was working. The businesses along the street had lost power, too. People were coming out of the buildings and gathering on the sidewalks.

"Then, I heard a woman screaming and saw her across the intersection, pointing up at the sky. Just seconds after that, there was a huge explosion somewhere to the west, in the direction of the airport. People started panicking and running up and down the streets in every direction. The ones who had seen what happened were saying a big jet had circled several times but was losing altitude rapidly before it just turned hard to one side and pointed nose down and crashed. Some people were yelling something about 9-11 and saying it was another terrorist attack.

"I didn't know what to think of all that, or what to do really. Like I said, I'm from out in the country and things are crazy enough in the city even in regular times to me. I didn't have anywhere to go and there was no way I could call and find out if my parents made it to Houston or not, so I just decided to stay right where I was for a while until I could make sense of what happened. I mean, the truck was all I had in New Orleans and the only place I had to go. I don't know a soul there.

"But then, I got to talking to the man who was in the car behind me at the red light when it all happened. He said he lived in Metairie and commuted to his office in downtown New Orleans every day. He was there after Hurricane Katrina and knew things were going to get bad real fast if the power stayed off. He was prepared this time, though. He had a big generator and plenty of emergency food and other supplies at his house. After I told him about my situation—how I didn't know if my parents were even alive and that I had to get back home and check on my sister—he insisted that I come by his place to at least get some supplies for my trip. His house was just a couple of miles away, so I got my bow, my hunting knife, my boots, and my camo out of the truck and walked back there with him.

"He was a nice guy and his wife was great, too. They tried to talk me into staying there a few days to wait and see what was going to happen with the power situation, but by the end of the day, we still didn't know anything. A lot of people were starting to say they had seen strange lights in the sky the night before, though, and, considering the extent of the damage, that it must have been caused by something like a solar flare. There was no way to get any news, and no one was coming into the city by vehicle or any kind of aircraft, so it didn't seem likely I would be able to get the truck running anyway, so there was no point in waiting any longer."

"You were lucky to have met some nice folks," April said, keeping her eyes on the road.

"I sure was. I wanted to start walking immediately, because I knew I had more than a hundred miles ahead of me. I decided to leave at night, figuring there would be fewer people out on the streets after dark and that I could cover ground faster that way. It was still soon enough after the blackout that most people hadn't figured out what was going on, so it wasn't as dangerous as it would be in another day or two. Those folks fed me well before I left. They had a big propane cooker and didn't want to let the fresh shrimp and vegetables they had on hand go to waste, so it was quite a feast. Then they gave me a couple of MREs, a bunch of energy bars, and all the bottles of water I could carry in my pack and stuff in the pockets of my hunting clothes. I've still got some of the energy bars left if you're hungry, by the way."

"I'm okay," April said. "I ate a bowl of cereal for breakfast this morning before I left. I grabbed a few cans and the rest of the bread and chips David and I had at the apartment. It's back there behind my seat if you want any."

"We'll have plenty of food at our place," Mitch said. "You can take some with you to Hattiesburg, too. I know Hattiesburg is no New Orleans, but there are still enough people there that I imagine there will be problems, especially with the food supply. What part of the city do David's parents live in?"

"Their house is near the university. His dad works there. It's in a quiet neighborhood back off of Hardy Street. I think it's pretty safe there."

"Probably for now," Mitch said. "But there must be 50,000 or more people in the area. When the groceries run out, if they haven't already, it will get dangerous there, too. You probably can't stay there for long."

"I can't think that far ahead right now," April said. "All that matters to me now is getting to my baby. Once

I get her in my arms, *nothing* is going to come between us!"

"I don't doubt that at all," Mitch said. "And you'll get there later today, if this car keeps running as good as it is now."

"I hope you're right about that. Hey, what was it like, walking that far at night? Weren't you scared?"

"Not really. I figured that was a lot safer than walking out in the open in broad daylight, even if I wasn't carrying anything that looked valuable. Even before what happened today, I already knew there was no telling what people might do when they got desperate. Besides that, I didn't want to get hassled by cops or anyone else for carrying the bow. I knew I would need it for hunting, and it was all I had for self-defense until I could get back home. That couple that fed me and gave me supplies agreed that it might be a good idea to get out that first night, if I insisted on going anyway. Most everyone else was scared and hunkered down, not knowing what was happening so soon after the blackout.

"I figured as long as I kept a low profile and kept to myself, I could likely get out of the city unnoticed. I stayed up on the Interstate all the way out of the city, because it's mostly elevated over some of the rougher neighborhoods it passes through. I made it almost to the Twin Span Bridge by daylight the next morning, then

I laid up for the day in the back of a UPS delivery truck, hidden among the packages. It was hot in there by mid-day, but I still managed to get some sleep. I started out again as soon as it was dark and got across the bridge and through Slidell the second night.

"I saw a few other people moving about at night while I was walking through the urban areas, especially that first night. Some were huddled in groups around their broken down cars, still waiting, still thinking authorities of some kind were going to come along and rescue them. I felt bad for them, but I couldn't do anything to help, and my responsibility was to get home to look out for my little sister.

"I walked as fast as I could during the nighttime hours with few breaks. I'm guessing I covered about twenty miles per night. It was easier to keep going at night, because it was so much cooler than in the day-time. By the third night, I was in Mississippi and got off the Interstate and onto Highway 11, just like you did, until I came to where the railroad ran beside it, then I walked on the tracks to make it even less likely I'd be seen. I started feeling better once I was out in the country again. I kept going this morning a while after daylight until I found that place back there where I had finally fallen to sleep till your car woke me up."

"You've got to be worn out then if you walked that far last night and have barely had any sleep."

"I'm okay. I'm used to walking a lot. I'm in the woods just about every day, all over our land and beyond it, too. It joins up to part of Desoto National Forest on one side. I can do all the roaming I want there."

"I can't imagine living in a place like that. I would get bored to death, I guess," April said. "I suppose I'm just a city girl at heart."

"I freakin' hate cities, and just about everything about them. Heck, I don't even like *towns.* I didn't want to go to New Orleans in the first place, but my mom's best friend—her old college roommate—died of cancer and Dad didn't want her to have to go to the funeral in Denver alone. I figured that as much as going to New Orleans sucks, it would beat sitting in school all day, and besides, dropping them off meant I would get to use Dad's new truck the whole time they were gone.

"Hey, speaking of New Orleans, is that where you're from? I know it's none of my business, but I was just curious about you having a kid and all. I mean, being on your own and all at eighteen." He sputtered, hoping he hadn't gone too far and tried to recover a little by saying, "You mentioned your dad. Where do your parents live?"

He glanced at her nervously. Even if she really was eighteen, like she'd said, she most likely had not finished high school before she got pregnant. He wondered if she had run away from home to live with her boyfriend. Maybe her parents didn't even know where she was? She sat thinking for a second, and just when it seemed like she was about to answer, she suddenly let off the gas and started to slow down, leaning forward over the wheel as if that would help her see better. The rain was heavy now, and the windshield wipers were having a hard time keeping up with it. Mitch turned his eyes back to the road to see what had gotten her attention.

"There's something going on up ahead, Mitch. It looks like a roadblock!"

FIVE

April slowed down to around ten miles per hour as she strained to see through the rain-smeared windshield. She had noticed a highway sign that indicated they were approaching a crossroads just before she was able to discern that the road ahead was blocked with a line of vehicles turned perpendicular to the lanes. Now that she was closer she could just make out another sign that showed the junction as Highway 26.

"I'm not surprised," Mitch said. "This little town has always been notorious for roadblocks and cops that like to throw people passing through in jail."

"I guess we'll just have to see what they want," she said nervously.

April fought to keep her panic in control. She felt more and more trapped the closer they got to the roadblock. She had a strong urge to just turn the car around and speed back the other way. But Kimberly was *this* way. She had to keep going north to Hattiesburg. Nothing else was more important. She stopped the Mustang ten feet away from the line of cars. Two men wearing police-blue ponchos and Western-style cowboy hats with plastic covers on them stepped out from behind the vehicle barricade. Each of them was cradling a long gun across his chest in one arm, while holding up the other hand in an unmistakable gesture that meant "STOP." April had learned enough about guns from shooting with her dad to know that one of the weapons was a riot shotgun like the kind most police departments owned and the other one was some kind of military short-barreled rifle or submachine gun. She was sure that, like all cops, they probably wore pistols on their belts, too, but she couldn't see them because of the ponchos. Both men looked serious, and she felt herself getting almost as tense as when the three men from the house approached her.

"Roll the window down," Mitch said. "They look like local town cops."

She did as he said, ignoring the rain that splattered on the doorsill and into the car. The one carrying the shotgun walked up to the open window, while the other held his position in front of the car, as if to cover him in case something went wrong. April fought back a panicked thought: *What if these officers had somehow found out she had killed a man back there on the road, and that her companion had killed two? Maybe they even thought the two of them had killed the older couple Mitch had seen inside the house?*

But then she got a hold of herself. *How could they possibly know what had happened back there already?* No one was around to see and even if someone did, they would not have been able to call anyone here unless maybe they had a two-way radio of some kind that was somehow still working. It was at least fifteen miles back to the house and no other vehicles had overtaken them on the road, nor had they even seen another running car.

"Well, what have we got here?" the officer asked, as he looked at her through the open window and then bent down to get a better view of Mitch in the passenger seat. "What are you two kids doing out on the road? Do you understand how dangerous it is to be traveling right now? And where did you get a running car, especially a classic Mustang? Did you steal it in New Orleans or somewhere?"

April didn't know which of this barrage of questions to respond to first. "We're going to Hattiesburg," she said, truthfully. "My baby is there, with her grandparents. I haven't seen her since the power went off. This is my fiancé's car."

"Fiancé? That boy there? I don't think either one of you looks old enough to be engaged, much less have a baby. Where are your parents? Are you running away from home or something because the power is out?"

"No, sir. *He's* not my fiancé. This is my friend, Mitch. My fiancé, *David,* is in Hattiesburg with our little girl, at his parent's house. I *am* old enough. I'm eighteen and my parents are both dead, so I can't really run away." She was aware of Mitch's surprise when she said this, but he kept quiet. The officer seemed completely unconvinced. He stood there, indifferent to the rain that splattered off his hat and poncho, and looked at both of them as if he were trying to decide whether to lock them up or not. Before she could protest, he reached for the door latch and opened the driver's side door.

"I'm going to have to ask you both to step out of the car, miss. Both of you, keep your hands up where I can see them, and walk around to the back of the car."

"But it's pouring!" April said.

"GET OUT! You won't melt. C'mon move it, I'm not going to ask you again!"

April knew there was no point in arguing with him now. At this last command, the other man, the one with the weapon that looked like a submachine gun, had brought his muzzle to bear in their direction, holding it at the ready with both hands as if he were just waiting for an excuse to use it. April did as she was told, climbing out of the seat. She put her hands up and stepped out into the rain, then moved to the rear of the car at the same time Mitch did.

"Don't tell them any more than we have to," Mitch whispered.

"Have you got any weapons in this car? What about dope? I'll bet I'm going to find something, so you'd better tell me now, because it'll be a lot worse on you if you say you don't and I find it anyway."

"I don't do drugs!" April said. "And neither does he!"

"We don't have any guns," Mitch said. "My bow and arrows are in the car, and I've got my hunting knife, but those aren't weapons." He kept quiet about April's knife, knowing she probably still had it in her pocket. "Look, I'm just trying to get back to my folks' place up in Perry County. I was stuck in New Orleans when the power went off. I walked most of the way until she offered me a ride. She's telling the truth, she's just trying to get to her baby in Hattiesburg."

"I'll decide what the truth is," the officer said. "First of all, I want to see some I.D."

April told him that her driver's license was in her small purse that she'd shoved under the driver's seat. Mitch said his was in his wallet, and the man directed him to remove it slowly and hand it over. He left them standing there in the rain and then sat down in the driver's seat of the car while the other man, who had moved around to the passenger side to keep them in view, covered them with his weapon at point blank range. Standing there in the rain, they were both soaked through in a matter of minutes while the officer inside the car seemed to be in no hurry as he rummaged through the interior. When he finally got back out of the car, he had Mitch's bow and quiver in one hand, as well as April's purse and the plastic grocery bag full of the food she'd brought from the apartment.

"I've got some questions for both of you," he said. "Take 'em over there to the store, Ladner," he said to the other officer. "Get 'em out of the rain. I'm going to check the trunk, and then I'll be right over there."

"But we have to go!" April said. "I *have* to get to Hattiesburg today!"

"You're not going anywhere until you answer some questions. Now go with him, out of the rain."

April looked at Mitch and he nodded. They had no choice. They walked the way the officer indicated, while the other followed behind them with his weapon at their backs. They squeezed between the vehicles forming the makeshift roadblock and crossed the intersection to a deserted convenience store on the other side. There was a large metal awning covering the self-service gas pumps, and a long bench probably used in normal times by customers who sat there drinking coffee and exchanging small-town gossip.

The officer ordered them both to have a seat. It was only another minute before the other one joined them, carrying Mitch's bow and quiver, which he propped against a soda machine beside the bench. April saw that he also had the bucket and the piece of hose Mitch had used to siphon the gas. He set those down on the pavement and held up their driver's licenses and some folded papers he had stuck in the plastic bag to protect them from the rain. He waved these in their faces as if they were somehow incriminating pieces of evidence.

"Okay, Mr. Mitchell Henley and Miss April Gibbs. I have the registration and insurance papers for one 1969 Ford Mustang right here, and I don't see either of your names on the paperwork anywhere. It seems this car belongs to a Mr. David Greene, of New Orleans, Louisiana. His address on these documents doesn't match the one on your license, Miss Gibbs. Now, do you want to tell me again what you are doing trying to drive through my town in Mr. Greene's car?"

"I *told* you the truth already," April said. "David Greene *is* my fiancé. It *is* his car. We weren't living together when I got my license, that's why the address doesn't match mine. That's my old address from when

I lived with my mother. He drove my car to Hattiesburg before the blackout to go pick up our baby, Kimberly, but when all the newer cars got shut down by this electric pulse thing, of course he couldn't get back. That's why I'm driving the Mustang there, because this is one of the few cars that will run."

The policeman said nothing. He had taken his plastic-wrapped cowboy hat off now that they were out of the rain, revealing a close-cropped military-style crew cut. The other one he'd called Ladner was still silently pointing his weapon at them. She guessed that the one asking them the questions was in charge; maybe he was even the chief of police. Whoever he was, he was obviously used to wielding his authority, even if his jurisdiction was nothing but a small south Mississippi town of a few thousand people. Before he spoke again, he picked up the bucket and the piece of hose he'd placed in it. "You want to tell me what you were doing with *this*?" He was looking at both of them when he asked the question.

"Sure," Mitch said. "I used it to siphon some gas, because when I met her, she had just run out and was stranded and alone in the middle of Highway 11."

"So, who did you steal the gas from, son? Did you just help yourself from somebody's car?"

"Just a few gallons, and it was an *abandoned* vehicle, like the hundreds that are abandoned everywhere. It's not like you can just buy gas anymore. I only took enough so we could get to my family's farm up in Perry County. We've got gas and diesel up there. I'm going to give her more when we get there, so she can make it the rest of the way to Hattiesburg."

"Stealing gas is against the law, regardless of the reason, son. I could arrest you both just for that, but I've got another question for you." He set the bucket down and then reached for the quiver of arrows. "I'd like to know what you've been shooting with those arrows, son. This is fresh blood."

He pointed to the matted, bloodstained fletching of the arrow Mitch had picked up out of the grass, the one that had passed completely through a man's neck. Although Mitch had wiped it off in the grass as best he could, there was still a lot of congealed blood in the feathers. As disgusting as it was to him, he had put it back in his quiver because he only had a few arrows and could not afford to waste it.

April could hardly breath and her stomach twisted into tight knots as she waited to see what Mitch would say. She wondered again if these policemen somehow already knew what had happened and had set the road-block up just for them, as they would in any circumstance to catch suspected murderers.

"It was a dog," Mitch said. "A wild dog. There was a pack of them. They ran out of the woods at me while I was walking down the railroad this morning. I killed one with that arrow and hit another one that ran off before the rest of them turned back and left me alone."

"How do I know you aren't lying about that, boy? How do I know you haven't just shot a deer out of season? What are you doing hunting this time of year anyway?" He was looking Mitch up and down, eyeing the head to toe camouflage.

"I wasn't deer hunting out of season, officer. My dad is a game warden up in Perry County. I *know* when deer season is. But I had my bow and gear with me in the truck because I hunt wild hogs year 'round on our land, and that's perfectly legal. If you've got a game warden here in town, he probably knows my dad. His name is Doug Henley. You know Perry County is just two counties over, east of here."

April began to breathe easier at this turn in the conversation. It was clear now that the policeman questioning them had not even suspected that Mitch had killed a *person* with his bow and arrows. He was just worried about whether he had broken some stupid wildlife law—as if that mattered in a situation where lots of people were probably going to have to kill whatever animals they could just to survive.

"Never heard of him," the man said. "You heard of a warden named Doug Henley, Ladner?"

"No, sir, but I don't keep up with the wildlife folks outside our jurisdiction. Ol' Warden Miller would know, but hell, I ain't seen him since the blackout."

"I'm not going to say you're not telling the truth about your dad, son. And I'm not going to confiscate your bow, even if you did kill a game animal out of season. I'm not even going to lock you up for stealing gas, even though you've admitted to it. I've got enough people around here already that are probably going to fill up my jail, so I'm going to let you two go. What I can't do, though, is let that Mustang leave here until I get some proof that it's not stolen."

"You have proof!" Mitch said. "You have the registration papers right there in your hand. She's telling the truth. The car belongs to her fiancé."

"How long have you two known each other, son? And do you know this Mr. David Greene? These papers show that the car belongs to him. They don't say nothing about her." The officer looked at April again, as if he were trying to see inside her mind.

"If you had a baby with the man that owns that car, miss, why aren't the two of you married? Didn't anybody ever tell you that you're supposed to get married *before* you have a child together? Now, if you *were* married, and this driver's license of yours showed that your last name was Greene, just like his, then I could let you drive that car away. But since you can't prove a thing, the car stays here until you come back with one Mr. David Greene to get it."

"You can't keep my car! I've *got* to get to Hattiesburg. You don't understand! I've got to get to my baby!"

"Like I said, I'm not stopping you from leaving, miss, neither one of you. You're free to go, and free to get your things out of the car." He made a sweeping motion with his hand out to the pouring rain beyond the edge of the awning, as if he were offering them the whole world. Then he handed back their driver's licenses, but not the car's registration papers or the keys that he had put in his pocket after searching the vehicle.

"You can't do this!" Mitch said. "*You* are the one stealing the car! You're taking our only transportation and putting us out on the road to walk in this weather? This is highway robbery!"

"You'd better shut up with your accusations while you're ahead, son! My jail might be filing up, but I could make room for two more if I wanted to. I could lock you both up right now and throw away the key until the lights come back on, and I will if you don't get out of my town before I change my mind. Things are falling apart everywhere, but my job is to protect and serve *my* community. *I'm* the one, the *only* one, who gets to make the decisions here about what's right and what's wrong, and as long as the grid stays down, I'm going to make the decisions that are in the best interests of the people here who trust me. If you two know what's best for you, you'll make tracks on down that highway right now and be thankful you've at least still got your freedom!"

SIX

April squeezed back through the roadblock behind Mitch as he led the way east on Highway 26 in the pouring rain. They had taken their few possessions from the Mustang—his small daypack, some of the remaining food she had brought from the apartment, and a small canvas tote bag she had stuffed some extra clothes in when she left. They had nothing to protect themselves from the weather, and the clothes they were wearing were already wet from standing out in the rain when they were first ordered out of the car. Now almost everything they had was wet, and there was no indication the rain was going to let up.

Before leaving the car, April did manage to line her canvas bag with one of the plastic grocery bags to at least keep one change of clothes somewhat dry. She was furious and bewildered at what had happened, but had given up trying to argue with the two men who had confiscated the Mustang. Everything she and Mitch said just made the situation worse, so they had to reluctantly walk away. Still, it was almost impossible for her to accept that they were not going to get the car back unless David came back for it.

"How could they do this to us? I can't believe something like this could happen in America. It's like we don't have any rights at all."

"We *don't* have any rights," Mitch said. "Because right now, the usual laws don't even apply. I guess we're essentially under martial law, which means anybody with a gun can pretty much do whatever they want. Those guys know they're in complete control of their town without any outside interference or higher authority to answer to, so they can just make up their own laws and do whatever they please as long as this lasts. They're kind of used to doing that around here anyway."

"A lot of stuff like this happened after Hurricane Katrina," April said, "and that was just a storm that shut things down in a limited area. Police were going around house to house in some places, confiscating people's guns, and they even caught some local cops in New Orleans stealing brand new cars from the dealerships. It's amazing what people will do when they think they can get away with it."

April stopped in the middle of the road as soon as they were out of earshot of the men at the roadblock. "We can't *let* them get away with it! I'm not letting them have David's car, just like that. I could be with my Kimberly today if we just had that car." She didn't budge until Mitch stopped and turned to face her.

"What do you think we can do?" he asked. "It's pretty clear that arguing with them won't do any good. Do you seriously think we can go up against them armed the way they are? Do you want me to try and sneak up on them and kill them with my arrows like those other two guys? Those guys were unarmed, and they never saw what hit them. They deserved to die for what they did and what they intended to do. These cops may be thugs, too, but we can't start fighting cops, or you will never get back to your baby and I'll never get to my little sister and my home."

"Of course I'm not suggesting we fight them or try and kill them. It's just that this is *so* wrong. There's got to be someone who can help us. Maybe if we find some other policemen or the sheriff or something?"

"I don't think that would do us any good. Look, these guys are not going to keep the car forever. He said you could have it back; you just have to have David along to claim it. I don't know what to tell you. I know it sucks, and it sucks for me, too, because I could have used a ride."

"I think they're just keeping the car so they can use it themselves. Their patrol cars are probably useless, so now they're just commandeering any running vehicle that someone tries to drive through their little redneck town."

"You're probably right, but there's no sense just standing here in the rain and talking about it. We're getting wet anyway, so we might as well keep walking."

"Walking where? You're walking back home to some land in the middle of nowhere. I've got to get to Hattiesburg. I don't even know how far it is from here, but I know it's going to take a long time to get there if have to walk the whole way."

"We don't have any choice right now but to walk, and I'll feel better if we get away from this town as soon as possible. It's up to you, but it would make more sense to stick together. From where we are right now, it's about the same distance to our family land as it is straight up Highway 11 to Hattiesburg. If you come with me, I can give you a ride from our farm as soon as I make sure my little sister is okay."

"A ride? How are you going to give me a ride?"

"We've got an old truck in the barn out behind the house. It's a '61 Ford that belonged to my grandpa. It doesn't get used much but it *will* run. I'll just have to air up the tires and hope the battery still has enough of a charge to turn it over."

April considered this as she walked alongside Mitch, who was already on the move as he was talking. She didn't like the idea of going so far out of her way to follow him home when that time could be spent walking straight to her Kimberly, but on the other hand, she didn't relish the idea of walking alone, either. It wouldn't make sense for him to walk out of his way to Hattiesburg with her with no prospect of getting back home other than to turn around and walk back, so she didn't even suggest it.

From what he said, his family land was sort of on the way, but somewhat east of the more direct route to Hattiesburg along Highway 11. If, and it seemed like a big if, the old truck he said was there would start and run, then maybe it made sense to go with him. After what happened this morning, she knew that two would have a better chance than one.

"What if the battery is not charged? What then? It's not like we can jump it off another car or something."

"There are other options," Mitch said. "My mom's car will be there at the house. Of course it won't run, because it's a late model Chevrolet, but we could take the battery out of it if we had to. Then there's my dad's tractor. The battery in it should be good. It may be slow, but it's a heck of a lot faster than walking. We have options, but I'm sure we can get the old truck running."

April made up her mind to trust this new friend she had just met hours ago, so she started walking alongside him. She let go of the idea of getting the car back with a sigh, and, like Mitch, she was now ready to leave this town behind as fast as possible.

They headed east on Highway 26 instead of continuing straight north on Highway 11 because the railroad tracks that ran roughly parallel to it were just a short distance away. It was the same railroad he'd been walking on before he met her, and he said it would be much safer than walking on any highway, especially until they got well away from the town and its outlying residential areas. April didn't argue with that logic, and when they came to where the highway crossed over the tracks, she followed him down the steep, muddy bank and they plodded north again along on the cross ties and gravel between the two rails as the rain poured down.

"One good thing about this rain is that even though it's hard to see far in it, it makes us just about invisible, too," Mitch said.

"We're probably the only ones dumb enough to be out here walking in it."

"Just think of it as camouflage. Once we get a few

miles north, we will turn off on the tracks onto one of the big pipelines. Then, we'll really be in the boondocks."

"Pipelines?" April couldn't really picture the idea of walking along a pipeline. It just wasn't something that had ever been on her radar in the cities she had lived in. Mitch explained that you didn't really see the pipeline itself, because it was buried underground, but each one was surrounded by a wide, cleared right-of-way that made for a reasonable walking route through otherwise trackless terrain. Most of the rural land in Mississippi was crisscrossed with such pipelines, the bigger ones running long distances into neighboring states in both directions, and the smaller ones tying into them from outlying oil or natural gas fields and remote pumping stations. They usually ran in arrow-straight lines for miles, up and down hills and across streams and rivers, over open farmland and through the heaviest forests.

While following them was sometimes tough, they had the great advantage of usually being out of sight of roads or houses. The only people who frequented them were the occasional workers clearing paths or doing inspections. During deer season, hunters sometimes used the long sight lines of the open right-of-ways to ambush their prey at a distance with high-powered rifles. April wondered if they, too, might be susceptible to such an ambush while traveling those routes, but Mitch felt confident that people out in the rural areas were going to be plenty busy with their immediate survival and would not likely be far from home roaming areas like the pipelines. At least not this soon after the lights went out.

"People out here in rural Mississippi tend to mind their own business anyway," Mitch said. "Unless you're threatening them or trying to steal something from them, you don't have anything to worry about out here."

"From what I've seen since I left New Orleans, I don't want to run into *any* other people. You're the only person I've met so far who hasn't wanted to take my car or kill me. I'm sorry the ride didn't work out. Helping me didn't get you very far, did it?"

"I'm not worried about that. I'm just glad I happened to be able to help. Hey, I'm sorry to hear about your parents . . ."

"What?"

"You told that cop back there they were both dead. Is that true?"

"Yeah, thanks. It was a long time ago when I lost my dad, then my mom a little more than a year ago. I'll tell you about it later."

They continued on in silence, each lost in their own thoughts as they made their way north. Walking on the big chunks of rock that made up the railroad bed was not easy on her feet, and April was glad she had at least put on a pair of comfortable cross-trainers before she left New Orleans that morning. Like everything else she had on, though, her shoes and socks were soaked through and through. With every step she could feel the water squish beneath her soles, and she wondered if she would have blisters by the time they quit walking.

Mitch had claimed he was covering around twenty miles per night those first three nights, and she thought that seemed like a long way to walk in one stretch. She had never tried it, if only because she'd never had reason to. But she was determined that if he could do it, then she could, too. She would do whatever it took to get to Kimberly as soon as humanly possible.

Like Mitch had said, the railroad tracks ran mostly out of sight of the roads, houses, and other buildings of the town, and sooner than she expected, they were back in the countryside. Like the pipelines he seemed to know so much about, the railroads were travel corridors she probably wouldn't have thought to use as a walking route, but it made a lot of sense, especially now that no trains were running and the roads were the routes almost everyone else would take. Mitch said he had often walked the tracks for miles while hunting or simply roaming the woods, as they led through areas inaccessible by regular roads, just like the pipelines do.

They hadn't seen another soul out here so far and now that they were well away from the town, she thought they likely wouldn't.

By late afternoon the rain was showing no sign of letting up, so Mitch suggested they try to find some shelter for the night. "There's no need to be miserable," he said. "It's bad enough walking in this weather in the daytime. I don't think we have to worry with traveling at night out here like I did closer to the city. Besides, we should be far enough north now that we can start heading east on one of the pipelines in the morning."

"That's fine with me. How about that underpass so we're out of the rain?" April said, pointing to a bridge over the tracks that was just visible in the distance.

"Okay, if that's just a small county road, like I think it is, we should be pretty safe there. It's possible someone might come along, but I doubt anyone will. We can take turns keeping watch. I've got to sleep some time. Before you came along and woke me up with your car, I probably had less than an hour of sleep. I need some rest and you do, too, because we will probably have a much longer and tougher hike tomorrow."

SEVEN

When Mitch and April walked under the shelter of the concrete overpass it was the first time they had been out of the rain since they left the roadblock hours earlier. He waited and listened for a few minutes to make sure there was no sound of activity on the road overhead. Then, keeping low and moving slowly, he climbed the steep bank to the roadway to have a look.

The road was the typical rural county route common all over the state: crushed gravel over asphalt with no painted centerline or any signage to indicate a name or number. Most of these roads didn't go over railroad crossings unless they had a fair amount of traffic, but there was no development or anything else but pine forests as far as he could see on either side of the pavement, and there were no stalled vehicles in sight.

Without a map, he had no way of knowing where the road went, as he was unfamiliar with this county aside from occasionally driving through it on the main high-ways. It appeared to run in a general east/west direc-tion, and could be a viable route to take them closer to their destination since they needed to travel east at some point, but he felt it would be safer to keep to his original plan and stay on the railroad until they crossed one of the larger pipelines. If they followed one of those to the east, they would have to cross a major stream called Red Creek, which he was sure he would recog-nize when he saw it, and continuing in that direction would eventually take them to U.S. Highway 49.

Satisfied that it was unlikely anyone had seen them approaching the overpass along the railroad, he felt that the prospect of a good night's rest out of the weather would be worth the small risk that someone might come along and discover them under the bridge before morning. He made his way back down the bank to where April waited. She was sitting on a concrete retaining wall under the overpass, out of the rain but obviously uncomfortable in her soaking wet clothes. At least she had something to change into if the grocery bags she was carrying her stuff in hadn't leaked. Mitch had nothing but what he was wearing, but he was too tired to care and figured he could sleep anyway.

"If you want to put on something dry, I'll climb back up there to the road and wait," he said.

April opened her bag and felt inside. "Okay, I do have another pair of pants and a T-shirt. I wish I had a sweatshirt or something, though. It's kind of chilly."

"Yeah, it's the damp. Can't get away from that, even under the bridge. I wish we could build a fire under here tonight, but it's just too risky. Tomorrow night we will probably be somewhere where we can."

"Well, it may be a damp under here, but I guess it's better than walking out in it all night."

Mitch knew she was anxious to keep moving and would probably be more than willing to walk all night in the rain if he would. But he was simply too tired, and besides, once they left the railroad, it would be difficult to find their way in the dark. He promised her they would get moving again at first light, whatever the weather conditions. He knew the rain was the least of her concerns.

He climbed back up to the road to give her some privacy to change, and as he stood looking in both directions to be sure they were still alone, he could only imagine the anxiety and anguish she must be going through. While he was worried about his little sister, the fact that Lisa was with friends in the small town where they all went to school eased his mind somewhat. He felt confident that she would be okay when he got there, and that being farther removed from big urban areas like New Orleans and even smaller cities like Hattiesburg and Gulfport, their community would not likely be inundated with a flood of refugees this soon after the blackout. He knew that could change, and expected that it likely would, but probably not before he got there and could take Lisa to the surer safety of their own land.

Lisa was thirteen and she was quite comfortable in the woods herself, even if she was not the fanatic about it that Mitch was. She had learned how to shoot and even hunted some with their dad, and already knew how to drive and could run the tractor almost as well. So, while it was his responsibility to look out for her for the duration of this crisis until their parents could return, she was far from the helpless one-year-old that April had to worry about.

While they were walking all afternoon in the rain, Mitch had more time to reflect on what had happened that morning. It was still almost surreal, but he had killed two men just hours before. He was surprised at how easy it had actually been, how he had spontaneously reacted to the situation as soon as he took it in and realized what was unfolding before his eyes. Despite his initial shakiness, his aim had been true and with just two perfectly placed arrows he had taken out both men before they could react.

Even though he was not technically an adult, his years of dedication to learning hunting and woodcraft skills gave him distinct advantages over most people in a situation like this. Walking long distances and enduring the discomforts caused by the weather on a day like today were nothing new to him, and, in a way, he enjoyed the challenge. But thinking on all this, he knew there were many others with little in the way of survival skills or knowledge who were desperate to get somewhere: back home, out of a hopeless place like New Orleans, or to their loved ones as April was doing. How many would die trying before the power, communications, transportation, and security could be restored? He had no idea, but he was sure the numbers would be staggering if it took as long as he feared.

Most people had no prospect of a safe place to retreat to, much less six hundred acres of remote woods bordering on tens of thousands of acres of undeveloped national forestland. Not only was his family's land far off any main routes, it was also abundant with natural resources such as timber and firewood, edible plants, and wild game. A clear, spring-fed creek wound it's way through, en route to the larger Black Creek, guaranteeing safe water, even in the absence of electricity to run the pump that pulled water from their well at the house. Mitch's mom was in the habit of keeping the pantry well-stocked with groceries. Living that far out meant driving to Hattiesburg for most shopping, so she always bought a lot at a time. Of course all the frozen food, including the deer and wild hog meat he had contributed to their two large freezers, would be a thawed-out, stinking mess, but more fresh meat could easily be hunted without leaving the property. Compared to most, he and his sister were by far among the lucky ones.

But what about all the others? What about April? She had proven she was tough enough to be a survivor, there was no questioning that, but where would she go? Where could she possibly go with her child, the child's father, and her grandparents that would be safe for all of them? Where could they find the essentials of food and shelter and medicine if needed? He assumed that at least in some places people would try to organize shelters, but unlike after a hurricane or other limited disaster, supplies would not be pouring in from other regions. How were the authorities going to handle desperate, hungry crowds? How many places like the town they had just left were going to start making up their own laws out of desperation for some sort of order? It was mind-boggling to consider.

He climbed back down to the railroad after a few minutes and found her wearing a dry pair of jeans and a white T-shirt, her wet, dark hair combed and pulled back in a neat ponytail. She had spread out the remaining food she had salvaged from the small stash of groceries she'd put in the car that morning, and Mitch sat down beside her to eat. They shared the last of a bag of tortilla chips and a jar of spicy salsa, and ate cold black beans right from the can.

"This sure beats those energy bars I've got left," Mitch said.

April was staring off into space as she ate. "I just wonder if Kimberly is getting enough to eat. I keep worrying that David had already left that morning with her in my car before the power went out," April said. "If he did, they might be outside somewhere just like this. They wouldn't have anything to eat, because he wouldn't have had any reason to bring food for what he thought was going to be a two-hour drive. It makes me sick to think about it. No one could properly care for a one-year-old out here like this, and especially not David."

"It happened so early," Mitch said, "like you said before, they probably hadn't left his parents' house yet."

"I can hope. At least I know for sure that David *does* like to sleep in whenever he can. He was supposed to go to work that day, but not until noon. So he knew he could wait and leave as late as nine in the morning and still get home in time. But even if they are both at his parents' house, I wonder if they're going to have enough to eat and how long they'll be able to stay there. I'm afraid for my baby. I'm afraid for all of us after what I've seen. What are we going to do?"

Mitch didn't have the answer. It would be much simpler if it were just her, alone as she was now. He would tell her to come back to his house and wait out the rest of this nightmare with him and Lisa. Her need to travel to Hattiesburg first was a problem. It would be dangerous going into any urban area, and dangerous getting back out, especially with a baby. There would be at least five of them, counting David's parents. How difficult would it be to provide for so many, in addition to meeting his own needs and those of his sister? What about Lisa's friends and others he knew from school and the town, who might also have difficulty surviving the duration of this event? Could he invite them all to his family's land? How many would there be, and what about other strangers, other refugees who might find their way there on their own? How many could he help, if any? How would he turn away the ones he couldn't, or even stop them all? And what of his own parents? Would his mom and dad be able to make their way back, and if so, how long would it take?

Mitch had a lot more questions than he had answers, but he had a lot of respect for this brave young woman (whom he still thought of as a girl his own age), and he was determined to help her however he could.

A week ago, he would have never dreamed he'd be sitting under a bridge in the middle of nowhere with someone like April. He had never met a girl anything at all like her, and as they ate and talked he found the opportunity to really look at her for the first time since they'd met that morning. With her wet, dark hair pulled back from her face, he could see that she was pretty without the eyeliner and mascara most of the girls he knew from school would not be caught dead without. She had a natural look that he found much more attractive, and her confidence and the ease with which she adapted to the circumstances they were in made her that much more appealing.

April was easy to talk to, and he was not intimidated by her even though he was usually extremely shy around girls, especially most of the ones from school. He found it hard to look them in the eye when he had a reason to talk to one, and he rarely started the conversation. He was an outsider to the circle of the popular kids, and the only girls he was even remotely attracted to were definitely in that clique. Since he didn't play the usual team sports or join in the unofficial extracurriculars, like sneaking off to the creek after school to drink beer or smoke pot with the rest of them, he was mostly excluded and kept to himself.

He had developed crushes on a couple different occasions for girls that a lot of the other guys in the school were into, but none of those girls had ever given him the time of day. He thought about one of them sometimes when he was alone in the forest, fantasizing that she had his same interests and was there with him, living a life of adventure in the wild, free of the classroom and the idiotic rules of school and society in general. Usually in these fantasies they were both warrior-hunters, living by the bow and roaming a boundless primeval forest like the characters in the novels and movies that inspired his daydreams. Of course, the real-life girl he put into this fantasy world had little interest in the woods and would be horrified at the thought of the life he imagined for her. But for Mitch, when he was alone on the hunt, moving stealthily through the forest with weapons little changed for countless millennia, it was hardly a stretch to put himself in the dream worlds he conjured from the images of those stories.

It was so improbable, but now here he was, sitting in the dark with a strong, determined young woman not so unlike those of his fantasies. Both of them hiding from a world gone mad, and both of them carrying weapons bloodied that very day in a fight for life or death. Mitch said nothing about any of this of course, but as they sat there talking, he couldn't stop thinking how strange it all was.

April was still wired, so when she volunteered to sit up and keep watch first while he slept, Mitch didn't argue. He curled up on the ground a few feet away, wet and uncomfortable, but glad that for the first night since he left New Orleans, he was not alone.

EIGHT

Mitch was sitting awake in the predawn stillness listening to the sound of light rain falling when April began to stir. They both took their turns keeping watch and sleeping, and now he was ready to get moving. As soon as she stretched and had a drink of water from one of the bottles they were carrying, she was ready, too. His clothes had not had time to completely dry out, but it didn't matter because they would soon be back out in the rain again anyway. He left her again for a few minutes so she could change back into her wet clothes, climbing back up to the roadway to look and listen.

Nothing was moving on the road, and even the usual sounds of the morning woods were hushed by the softly falling rain. As the sky began to lighten, a solitary squirrel barked from somewhere in the mist-cloaked woods nearby, but he could hear no evidence of human life besides their own. The complete absence of mechanical sounds was amazing. Mitch was used to quiet mornings in the deep woods on the farm, but even there or in the farthest reaches of Desoto National Forest, there was almost always some faraway sound of traffic on a highway, an outboard motor on the creek, or a passing plane overhead. Now, all of that was gone. The silence in the absence of humanity's machinery was palpable.

Mitch had only experienced this kind of quiet once before, when his dad had taken him elk hunting two years ago in the Bitterroot Mountains of Montana, one of the few truly wild places remaining in the Lower 48. If there was anything good that came out of the failure of the modern world, this silence was it—at least while it lasted.

For breakfast they finished off the rest of April's canned black beans and ate two of the remaining energy bars that the couple in New Orleans had given him. Mitch told her that he thought it would take two full days to get to their land, partly because of the weather and partly because traveling cross-country along a pipeline would be slower going. They probably had enough food to make it, but he said that he was going to be ready if any game that could be taken down with the bow presented itself. He carried the strung bow loosely in his left hand as they walked, the quiver of arrows slung over his shoulder along with his small daypack.

"Mornings like this, when it's just raining lightly, are actually some of the best days to hunt," he said. "If it's raining harder, deer and other animals don't move much, but in this, especially after a day of hard rain like yesterday, they are out looking for something to eat. It's easier to sneak up within bow range, too, because when the leaves and stuff are wet you can walk more quietly. The rain also helps hide our human scent."

"You're really into hunting, aren't you?"

"Nothing I'd rather do," he said.

"I guess there's not much else *to* do when you live way out in the woods, is there?"

"It's not quite like that," he said. "We do have a real house. We've even got TV and the Internet, if you can believe that!"

"*Did* have," April corrected him. "So, are you going to shoot a deer this morning?"

"No, we're way too far from home to carry a whole deer back, and I don't like to waste any part of an animal I kill. I'm not really hunting, because we've got a lot of ground to cover. It's just that if we come up on a rabbit or squirrel or something in easy range, I wanted to let you know so you wouldn't freak out if I suddenly pull out an arrow and draw the bow."

"Okay, I gotcha. Don't worry about me. I can be quiet if I need to."

They didn't have to walk much more than an hour before they saw what Mitch was looking for: a major pipeline crossing the railroad at a near perpendicular angle, running east and west. It was obviously one that would go to Highway 49 and well beyond, judging by the size of the well-maintained right-of-way path, which was probably 150 feet wide. Looking east along its route, they saw that it crossed rolling terrain of hills and hollows, unlike the well-graded railroad bed that was mostly flat.

"This looks like our turn off," Mitch said. "Like I said, the going won't be as easy, you can see that. It's going to be muddy everywhere, and we'll probably have to wade creeks down in some of those hollows."

"As long as it gets us to your place and I get to Hattiesburg, I don't care what we have to go through," April replied.

"You've got the right attitude," Mitch said. "You remind me a lot of my little sister. She's a tough girl.

"Well, at least it looks like the rain is letting up." He pointed to the sky back to the west. The clouds were much lighter and there was only a drizzle that seemed to indicate the rain front had passed over. By the time they had walked a mile or so east along the pipeline right-of-way, the rain had stopped completely. Both sides of the clear-cut swath were bordered by mature pine forests. The right-of-way itself was mostly covered in grass that was almost waist-high, with occasional patches of blackberry briars on the hillsides and river cane and small willows in the hollows. There were old tire ruts from the service trucks and ATV trails winding along the route most of the way, but in some places they had to push through thickets where there was no path. There were no signs that anyone had been along the route since the rain, which Mitch said would have washed out tracks left before it started.

"This is deeper into the middle of nowhere than I've ever been," said April.

"Well, this area isn't nearly as remote as our land. We've got a lot more of the national forestlands east of 49. That's were the Black Creek Wilderness Area is and there are several tracts of thousands of acres of woods with no roads of any kind."

Just thinking about those places made Mitch feel better. He was much more relaxed, now that they were surrounded by woods, and the closer he got to his familiar stomping grounds, the better he would feel. It also made him feel good that April trusted him enough to follow him there. It was a new experience for him and his outdoorsman skills to be so valuable and relevant when before they just made him an outsider to most everyone else his age. He was determined to show her that he was worthy of her trust, and as they walked he pointed out various animal tracks and other signs, such as droppings and deer runs. It was all new to her, and he delighted in sharing his knowledge with someone who seemed genuinely interested.

They followed the pipeline all day, crossing several gravel roads and a couple of small paved ones but seeing no one as they made their way east. The rain seemed to be gone for good, but the skies remained overcast, gloomy and gray with no sunshine to dry the saturated ground and vegetation of the forest. Mitch estimated they had covered fifteen miles or more by late afternoon. They took a short break about every two hours, but otherwise they walked mostly non-stop. He was starting to think about looking for a place to camp for the night as they started up another hillside after crossing a muddy low spot in the right-of-way.

Suddenly, something burst out of a clump of thick grass in front of him and took off up the path ahead. He froze in place and with one hand behind him, motioned for April to do the same. Then, with a deliberate, fluid movement that seemed to take forever in slow motion, he reached for an arrow with the same hand while the rest of his body remained motionless. When the arrow was free of the quiver, he brought the bow up with the other hand, careful to avoid any fast or jerky movement, while hoping that April was keeping still behind him. The rabbit they had spooked had done what rabbits frequently do when startled: it ran about a dozen yards and then stopped, its large ears erect, nostrils sniffing as it looked at them and tried to figure out what they were. Mitch drew the bow and steadied his breathing as he willed the rabbit to stay where it was for just a few more seconds, knowing that it could disappear in a flash if he hesitated too long. As soon as he felt his right thumb anchor to the spot on his cheek that told him he was at full draw, he released the string.

"You got him!" April said, in a loud whisper.

Mitch smiled at her and walked ahead, not bothering to draw another arrow, as it clearly was unnecessary. A broadhead of course wasn't ideal for small game, but all the arrows he had with him were fitted with those points because wild hogs were the only game legal to hunt that time of year. Its effect on a rabbit-sized animal was destructive, but also instantaneous, and it had died without a twitch.

"Ever eaten a rabbit before?" he asked her as he bent to pick it up.

"No, but I'm okay with it, I guess. As long as it's cooked."

"Of course. I think we can safely build a fire tonight since we're not near a road. If you're ready, I'd say we ought to start looking for a place to do that and get set up to spend the night. At least it's not going to rain any more."

Mitch led the way until the pipeline right-of-way reached a small crest, and then turned off along the ridge into the adjoining pine forest until he found a suitable area among the trees that was clear of under-brush and briars. "I think we'll be fine just sleeping out in the open tonight," he said. "If we get enough firewood together before it gets dark, we'll have enough to last all night."

Since the ground and any fallen branches that were on it were still soaked from the rain, Mitch showed April the old Indian trick of collecting "squaw wood," the smaller dead branches still attached to the lower reaches of standing live trees. He explained that these branches didn't soak up much water, since they were off the ground, and they were also generally harder than the half-rotten ones that had fallen off long before.

They collected a big pile in just a few minutes, as it was clearly not a place where anyone had camped before so there was a vast supply of available wood. A lot of it was still damp around the outer bark, but Mitch used his hunting knife to split some of the drier branches to get at the bone-dry wood inside. Once he had enough kindling, he collected dry pine needles and slivers of bark in the same way, and fished in his pack for one of the butane lighters he always carried while hunting.

Once the fire was going, he left April to tend it and walked off some distance to skin and dress the rabbit. He was looking forward to freshly roasted meat after so many days of travel on a mostly carbohydrate diet. When he had the animal quartered and ready, he cut a couple of small green saplings with forked branches and sharpened the ends to make skewers for the meat. He returned to the fire and gave one to April, letting her hold her share in the flames while he held his own.

"Kinda ironic, I guess; the game warden's son poaching rabbit out of season, isn't it?" Mitch sighed.

"I'm sure your dad would understand, given the circumstances. He must love wildlife to do that job, right?"

"He does. He loves everything about being in the woods. I reckon that's where I got it. He sure taught me most of what I know, although he's not nearly as into archery as I am."

"You're good with it all right. I've never seen anybody shoot a bow like that, except in movies, of course. Is it hard to learn?"

"Not the basics. It takes a lot of practice to get consistent with it, but I guess anything's like that. Have you ever shot a bow before?"

"Never. I would like to try it, though."

"Sure. Maybe tomorrow when we take a break somewhere, and you can at least get a feel for it. This bow I'm carrying is based on the medieval English longbow, which is widely regarded as one of the best designs ever, at least before modern technology and all those contraptions they make now called 'compound' bows that are really just arrow-shooting machines. Might as well use a gun as use one of those. I'm into this for the traditions of mastering a primitive weapon. I have a couple of Native American–style bows that are really cool, too."

As they talked they turned the roasting pieces of rabbit, and the afternoon faded to twilight by the time the food was done. Cooking it this way, it was inevitable that the meat would be charred on the outside, but Mitch assured April it would be delicious anyway, though he regretted not having any seasoning to put on it. When it was sufficiently burnt-looking, he cut into all the pieces with his knife to make sure they were done on the inside, and they began to eat.

"This is pretty awesome!" April said as she chewed the first bite.

"Yeah, wild rabbit is one of the tastiest game animals of all," Mitch said. He felt a deep satisfaction that she was pleased, and the pride of a hunter who has provided necessary meat. This would fuel his fantasies even more: a successful hunt with a primitive weapon, a fire in the darkening forest, its flames lighting the face of a beautiful woman. Mitch had dreamed of such things but never expected them to happen. He wanted the moment to last as they shared the meal in a scene that could come from somewhere at the dawn of humanity, before the first plow was invented or the first seed planted, when all men and women lived from the bounty of the forest.

Suddenly a loud crack that could only come from a high-powered rifle shattered the dream. They both dropped their food in a panic, and Mitch leapt across the fire, grabbing April in his arms and pulling her down with him as he flattened himself to the ground. His ears were still ringing with the report of a shot fired at close range as he lifted his head enough to scan their surroundings. The shooter was close, *really* close, and he found out how close when he saw a man step out from behind a large pine tree between their camp and the pipeline just a short distance away. The man held a scoped deer rifle at hip level, pointed right at them, and he yelled as he started walking closer: "WHAT THE HELL ARE YOU TWO DOING HUNTING ON MY LAND?"

NINE

The thunder of the rifle came so suddenly out of the stillness and fading daylight that the sound didn't register in her brain at first, but Mitch's reaction quickly brought her to the reality that once again they were in danger. She felt a rush of adrenaline when she heard the shooter yell his questioning accusation, and she pulled clear of Mitch even as he was beginning to get to his feet to face this new threat. Looking in the direction of the voice, she saw a man step into the firelight from the dark woods, his rifle leveled and menacing as he walked closer. It was clear that he was upset about their presence on what he was claiming was his land, and apparently he had fired the first shot to make sure he had their full attention. Now he was coming closer to either ask more questions or to ensure he would not miss when he shot again.

"We're just passing through," Mitch said. "I didn't know we were on private land here. We've been walking the pipeline, heading east. I didn't see any posted signs."

"Well it damned sure *is* posted! I don't need any signs. My house is just across that hollow there on the next ridge. I own all this land whether this damned Gulfsouth pipeline goes through it or not."

As he stepped closer, April could see that the man was middle-aged with graying hair showing under the edges of his baseball cap and a bulging midsection that was impossible to hide under his dark sweatshirt. The leather sling on the rifle he carried hung loose as he pointed the weapon at Mitch from waist level.

"I'm sorry," Mitch said. "We didn't know. I didn't see a house or know there was a road anywhere near here. I don't have a map. We're just trying to go east on the pipeline to get across 49. My family owns land over on Black Creek. I wouldn't mess with anything on anyone's private land. We just didn't know."

"Well, you damned sure should have known! You knew it wasn't *your* land. What's that you've killed there, a rabbit? You're stealing food right off my family's table by killing game on my land. I'm not about to tolerate any trespassing after what's happened this week. I'm about ready to start shooting anybody I see out here on sight, especially poachers from some city coming out here acting like they own the place."

He moved the muzzle of his rifle closer to Mitch's chest and told him to step back, away from where the bow and quiver of arrows were propped up on a log beside the fire. Then he kicked them aside with enough force that April wondered if the bow would be broken. When he turned to her, he ordered her to get to her feet as well. She did as she was told and he stepped closer, shoving his rifle barrel into her stomach, just above the navel.

"Leave her alone," Mitch said. "She didn't kill the rabbit, I did."

"Shut up! Both of you are trespassing." He turned his attention back to April and looked her up and down. "Where are you from? I know you're not from anywhere around here."

April didn't answer. She was fed up with being threatened and having guns pointed at her. But it was different this time. This was just one man, with one gun and no badge, and he had made the mistake of getting too close. With the end of the rifle at contact range, touching her body, she knew that all she had to do was get out of line with the barrel before he could pull the trigger, and with the bolt action rifle, he would only have time to fire one round. She had drilled this very thing countless times with her dad, often just playing around, but in serious training, too. It could be accomplished by either moving the barrel itself, moving her body out of line with it, or a combination of both. It would be suicide to try it if he were even one or two paces away, but touching her with the muzzle as he was doing, he unknowingly gave up all the advantages he had of having a gun in the first place.

It was obvious that this was probably the first time he had ever held someone at gunpoint, and he was letting his anger get the best of his judgment. She sized him up as these thoughts went through her head. He was clearly out of shape and, without a gun, probably wouldn't have the nerve to confront anyone. He was certainly not as intimidating as any of the three in the group that attacked her on the road. April made her decision. She looked in Mitch's direction and feigned a startled expression as if he were the one up to something. It worked. The man followed her gaze, taking his eyes off of her just long enough to give her time to act.

April pivoted her entire body ninety degrees as she stepped forward with her right foot, the sudden rotation moving her out of line with the rifle barrel as she simultaneously parried and grabbed it near the muzzle with her left hand. At the same time, she brought her right arm across in a vertical inward block so that her forearm smashed into the back of the man's extended left elbow, locking out his arm and nearly dislocating it as she maintained control of the barrel with her left hand. This push-pull motion, combined with the solid planting of her body into a horse stance with her right foot between both of his, immediately pulled the man off balance. He bent over at the waist, completely caught off guard by her sudden movement. He did not even manage to get off the single shot that would have missed her anyway, as he had taken his finger off the trigger.

With her forward step-through, April's right foot was in the perfect position for the lifting heel kick that came next, smashing straight up into his groin as she pivoted her upper body even more. Upon impact, the man relinquished his grip on the rifle, even before her knee cocked to follow up with a smashing back kick to his left inner thigh. She could have as easily directed the last kick into his knee instead, resulting in a crippling injury, but it wasn't necessary. He went down instantly and was crumpled on the ground in agony from the groin kick. April took another step away to create distance as she turned the rifle on him in case he tried to get back up. She glanced at Mitch and saw that he was speechless.

"I've about had enough of guns being pointed at me!" she said.

"Are you crazy? You could have gotten us both killed!"

"But I didn't, did I? You don't know what he would have done if we had done nothing."

Mitch picked up his bow and drew an arrow from his quiver, nocking it on the string just in case. He stepped closer to where she was guarding the fallen man with the rifle. "Have you ever used one of those?"

"Of course," she said. "Why don't you look around, make sure he is alone? He's not going to try anything else."

April was pleased with herself as she backed up to the fire, keeping the man covered while Mitch slipped away quietly with his bow to the pipeline to make sure there was no one else around. She had never disarmed a gunman in real life before, but in this case she had been confident she could do it. After what she had already been through, she realized she was going to have to stay up on her martial skills. The man on the ground was slowly catching his breath as he lay there bent in a fetal position with both hands between his legs.

"I didn't want to have to hurt you," April said, "but you asked for it when you shoved a gun in my belly."

He looked up at her, his face still twisted in pain. "I . . . I wasn't going to shoot you or anything. I'm just trying to keep people off my land."

"Mitch *told you* we were just passing through. We have a long way to go and we were just camping for the night and planning to leave at first light. People have been threatening me or trying to kill me or take my stuff ever since I left New Orleans, and I'm tired of it. We wouldn't be walking through here at all if some thieving cops hadn't taken my car."

April looked up as Mitch stepped back into the circle of firelight. It was almost fully dark now, and the forest was closing in around them. But with the skies clearing and an almost full moon rising over the right-of-way of the pipeline, Mitch had been able to see quite well out in the open. "There was only one set of tracks in the mud besides ours. It looks like whoever made them came from where he says his house is. I think he is alone."

"I *am* alone," the man said, looking up at Mitch. "I'm just looking out for my family. Ever since the blackout, I've been walking my property lines to check things, and I always carry my rifle, in case I see a deer. When I came up the pipeline over there, I saw your fire; that's how I knew you were here."

"Yeah, I can't believe I was that stupid," Mitch said, looking at April. "I'll be more careful about checking out the area next time we camp." He turned to the man on the ground, who was now sitting up, apparently feeling a little better as he recovered from the kick.

"Like I told you," Mitch said, "I'm a landowner, too, well my dad is, anyway. I'm sorry about the rabbit, but I thought we were on timber or oil company land or something instead of somebody's homestead. We haven't crossed a road in a while and haven't seen or heard any people."

"My place is at the end of a long gravel road," the man said. "You wouldn't have heard anything. Like I told your girlfriend here, I wasn't going to shoot either one of you. I just can't take any chances. I've got a wife and two kids at my house depending on me to protect them. You never know what people are going to do after what happened. I thought we were far enough out in the country to not have to worry about people coming through here, but I guess not."

"We're traveling the pipeline because it's safer than walking down the road. And she's not my girlfriend, but April here has already been attacked on the road. That's how we met."

"Well, I guess whoever attacked her got a surprise," he said as he looked back at April. "Where did you learn those moves? Crap, I never saw what hit me! I guess I won't make the mistake of underestimating a young girl again."

"The mistake you made was getting too close," April said. "If you're going to point a gun at someone, you don't give it to them by shoving it right against their body."

"Just be glad all you got was a kick in the balls," Mitch said. "The three men who attacked her back on Highway 11 are all dead."

April glared at Mitch to shut him up. She couldn't believe he would run his mouth about *that*. The man on the ground started to say something, but she cut him off. "He's just kidding," she said. "What's your name?"

"Mark, Mark Rainey."

"I'm April, and this is Mitch."

"Do you know if this pipeline goes all the way across Highway 49, Mark?" Mitch asked.

"Oh yeah. It goes all the way through Mississippi and I think across Alabama to Georgia. This is a major Gulf-south gas line."

"Good, I thought so."

"Where are you headed?"

"Not that far, just across 49 and then we'll work our way to the north. My family's land is up around Black

Creek right on the Perry County line, between Brooklyn and Janice Landing, if you know where that is."

"I know about where it is," Mark said. "That's a long way to walk."

"Not nearly as far as I've already come," Mitch said. "So, have you been out here at your place the whole time, ever since the pulse hit?"

"Yes. Thank God I rode my Harley in to work that day. I manage an auto parts store in Purvis. It's only about fifteen miles from here. I picked up my oldest boy from the elementary school and headed home right after it happened. My wife doesn't work, and my younger one is just three years old. We were pretty well set with supplies and have been keeping it that way ever since Katrina, when the power was off here for almost a month. I haven't gone anywhere except to ride the bike a few miles and check on some neighbors closer to town."

"You must have one of the older Harleys," Mitch said.

"I do. It's an old FXR. I bought it brand new in 1976 and have kept it well maintained. Best machine I've ever owned, and I'm sure glad I didn't sell it now."

April was still holding the rifle as they talked, not quite sure where things were heading as Mitch made conversation with Mark, telling him about David's Mustang, how she had put the carburetor back together by herself, and then how they had lost the car to the militant cops at the roadblock.

"That doesn't surprise me at all," Mark said, "especially at a time like this. Even in normal times, I'd drive fifty miles out of my way to avoid that town. The police there have always acted like the Gestapo."

"That's what my dad always said."

"Look, I'm sorry about pointing another gun at you two. I got what I deserved, and I'm lucky that you two are good people and didn't kill me for it. I know I overreacted, but this situation has really made me nervous, having to look after and protect my family all on my own out here. I guess we're so isolated I just expected the worst when I saw your fire and realized strangers were on my land. You're welcome to go ahead and camp here tonight, but I need to get back home. My wife would have heard my rifle shot, and she's probably worried about me still being out here so long after dark."

April gave him back his rifle, but not before working the bolt four times to eject the remaining cartridges from the magazine.

"I'm sorry about your ammo, but I can't just hand a loaded gun back to someone who just pointed it at me," she said, as she stooped to pick up the cartridges and slip them into her pocket.

"Oh, I *completely* understand, and that's the smart thing to do. Don't worry about it. I've got plenty more ammo for this rifle back at the house. Anyway, whether you stay here tonight or not, I wish you both the best of luck. Be careful and don't ever let your guard down. Hopefully this situation will be resolved before too many more people get hurt." With that, he turned and disappeared back into the dark in the direction from which he'd come.

"*That* was interesting," April said.

Mitch just looked at her like she was insane. "I'll say. I can't believe what you just did. That was amazing. You've got a lot of explaining to do. I've never seen anyone move like that. But first, let's get the hell out of here."

"Now?"

"Yeah. The moon is almost full. It's plenty bright out there on the pipeline. I'll feel a lot better if we put a few miles between us and this place before we sleep."

"You don't trust him, do you?"

"I don't trust *anyone*. Do you?"

TEN

Before he put the fire out, Mitch picked up the skewered pieces of rabbit they had dropped. After brushing off the leaves and grit, he and April quickly finished them off. Then they pulled the larger pieces of wood out of the flames and kicked piles of the sandy soil over the coals to smother them. With an arrow nocked on his bow at the ready, he led the way out of the dark pine grove to the moonlight-bathed opening of the pipeline.

At the top of the next ridge, a faint light through the woods proved to him that Mark had been telling the truth about living nearby. A bit farther along, the pipeline passed closer to the light and from there they could see that it was coming from the window of a house— probably an oil lamp burning inside. The pipeline did not cross a road in the vicinity, so it appeared that the house was at the end of a dead-end lane coming in from the north, just as Mark said it was. As they paused for a moment, April whispered that the man was probably honest, and wouldn't likely have come back to bother them.

Mitch was aware that breaking camp and moving like this in the darkness might be an overreaction, but being surprised by a rifle fired in such close proximity by an unseen shooter had really shaken him up. He didn't want that to happen again, and he was determined to make every effort to stay invisible for the rest of the journey. He should have known better than to build a fire so close to a potential travel corridor like a pipeline. They needed to eat, and the rabbit had to be cooked, but he had been careless by not moving farther from the right-of-way first. He had dropped his guard while they were eating, letting himself get wrapped up in the meal and conversation with April, oblivious of what was going on around them. This would have never happened had he been alone and fully alert. He couldn't believe he had been so stupid. Mark was hardly a woodsman, and despite being out of shape and clumsy, he had crept within a few yards of their camp without Mitch knowing it. He could have blown their heads off just as easily as he fired that warning shot.

Mitch didn't like that he made a mistake like that. He took pride in his abilities as a hunter and even though he'd successfully provided dinner, he had utterly failed at an even more important aspect of woodcraft and let an armed stranger get the drop on him and his new friend. He had been helpless in the face of Mark's rifle, while April on the other hand had almost effortlessly disarmed the man and put him on the ground, completely turning the tables.

Mitch was still in disbelief at what he'd seen her do, and kept replaying it in his mind as they walked. He had only seen that kind of stuff in movies, where invariably martial arts techniques were embellished and showy, with high kicks and dramatic acrobatic maneuvers. What April had done was smooth, efficient, and incredibly effective. There was nothing flashy about it and even from the point of view of a bystander, it was hard to tell exactly what she had done. It must have been even more confusing to be on the receiving end of it.

His first thought when it happened was that she was being reckless and taking a risk that could have gotten them both killed. But seeing how cool and collected she was after the man was down, Mitch realized she knew exactly what she was doing and had total confidence that she could pull it off. Seeing her grace under pressure helped explain how she'd taken out the first of the three men who had attacked her on the highway. He had been too far away when that happened to really see what she'd done, but it was clear to him now that there was far more to it than just random luck, and despite what she'd said, the training she'd done with her father must have been anything but casual.

They put a couple more ridges and hollows between them and the house when they came to a sizable creek in the next bottom. It was several yards wide and bordered by deep drifts of moonlit white sand that glowed in stark contrast to the dark rushing water. Wading was the only option for crossing it, unless they wanted to go well out of their way to look for a downed tree lying across it at a narrow spot, but it was too dark to go searching in the woods for that. Mitch took off his boots and led the way, finding it mostly knee-deep, except for one channel midstream where it came up over his waist.

"I'm pretty sure this is Red Creek, or at least a tributary of it," he said, when they were both across. "We can sleep somewhere on this side, and I'll feel a whole lot better knowing it's unlikely we've been followed. Tomorrow, we should reach Highway 49 easily. From there, all we have to do is make our way northeast, and we will eventually come to Black Creek. It runs roughly parallel to this one and they join together about a hundred miles downstream, but they're a long way apart in their upper reaches."

They found a place in the woods just up the next ridge from the creek. Mitch wanted to get far enough away from the running water so that the sound wouldn't drown out the noise of someone approaching, but he wanted to stay close enough to refill their water bottles in the morning without backtracking too much. Afraid to risk another fire this close to the pipeline, they sat in the dark, with just enough dappled moonlight filtering through the trees that they could make out each other's form but not see facial expressions as they talked. They were both too wired to fall asleep immediately, so Mitch began asking the questions he had been suppressing the entire time they were walking since Mark surprised them.

"My dad died when I was fifteen," April said. "It was completely unexpected. I mean, he was in phenomenal shape for a forty-year-old man, still working out every day, practicing martial arts, running. Then he just had a heart attack one morning at work, and he was gone before the ambulance could even get him to the hospital. My mom and I were shocked. Everyone who knew him was. It was one of those bizarre things no one would have ever expected."

"Was it some kind of hereditary heart condition or something?"

"Yeah, that's what the doctors said. Dad never knew he had a problem, because he was so fit. He never got sick, so he never went to a doctor."

"I'm sorry you had to go through that. You must have been close to him, to have learned so much about martial arts from him as young as you were."

"I was. It was the worst thing that ever happened to me up until that time, but I later found out that things could get much worse. My mom didn't take it well at all. She started changing about six months after Dad died. She started drinking, and she was taking other stuff—something she got from her shrink—and who knows where else. Less than a year after Dad was gone she started dating other men. I was furious about it, but she didn't let that stop her. She went from one to another, and she got so wrapped up with some of them that I was pretty much on my own most of the time. It got to where she didn't even come home some nights. I learned how to take care of myself. I cooked my own meals, did my laundry, walked to school . . ."

"That's rough," Mitch said. "Were you living in New Orleans then?"

"Yeah, we moved there right after Dad died, because Mom knew someone there who could get her a job in an insurance office. Before that, we had lived in San Antonio. That's where my dad worked.

"Anyway, this went on for almost two years. I tried to talk to Mom and I kept hoping she would come back around and be her old self, but she didn't. I didn't like any of the men she dated. None of them were anything like my dad, and I knew that none of them were any good for her. Then one night, she was riding home from some party with her newest boyfriend, and both of them had been drinking too much. He ran a red light at an intersection right in front of a big truck, and she didn't make it."

"I am so sorry, I can't imagine going through all that. I can't imagine losing one parent, not to mention both."

"It's okay. I got through it. Thankfully, I had David when that happened. I had not known him for very long, but after Mom's funeral and everything was settled, I moved in with him. I turned seventeen two months later, and Kimberly came along four months before my eighteenth birthday. We didn't intend for that to happen of course, but having her gave me a whole new reason to live.

"But I didn't mean to go into all that. You asked about the training. Yeah, I guess it was more serious than I told you before. I started taking it more seriously *after* Dad died anyway. He taught me everything I knew, but while he was there, I took it for granted that he would always be around to teach me more. After he was gone, practicing the forms and techniques he taught me felt like a way of connecting to his spirit. I could sometimes feel him with me as I went through the motions, especially when I really focused on what I was doing. I trained harder and harder, becoming pretty obsessed with it, at least during that time when Mom was still alive but not really there for me. Later, when Kimberly came along, I slacked off. I just didn't have the time, and I didn't need it in the same way anymore. I'm surprised I still remembered enough to make it work so well, to tell you the truth."

"Well, you sure made it work, and exceptionally well, I'd say. Was that Aikido or some kind of karate? Didn't you say your dad studied Aikido and something else?"

"Yes, Aikido and Shorin-ryu when he was living in Okinawa. Those are more traditional arts. When he came back here later on, he switched to a style called Kenpo, which is a blend of some of the best of the Chinese and Japanese traditional styles. That's mostly what he taught me. It's designed to be a modern method of hand-to-hand combat that's very effective on the street."

"Or the on the highway or in the middle of the woods!" Mitch said. "I never knew karate and stuff like that could really work so well. I've always wanted to learn how to fight like that, but growing up out in the middle of nowhere, there are no instructors."

"Tell you what, Mitch. I'll be glad to show you a few moves in exchange for a couple of lessons with that bow, if we have time, that is."

"You got a deal!"

Talking settled them both down enough so that they were finally able to get some sleep, and they passed the night undisturbed until they were awakened the next morning by birdcalls and chattering squirrels. It was going to be a clear, sunny day for the first time since he'd met April, and Mitch knew they would be able to cover a lot of ground that day.

He went back down to the creek they'd crossed before stopping for the night and searched the banks until he found what he was looking for—a seep spring welling up out of clay—a pure source of drinking water from which he could refill their water bottles without worry. Finding safe drinking water was rarely a problem along the creeks where such springs were common, but by following the pipeline they would have to cross long stretches of higher ground through barren pine forests. He was glad for the bottles as it was too far between water sources to walk without carrying at least a small supply.

They were on their way east again just as the dawn gave way to bright sunshine lighting the way ahead. Mitch said he hoped they would get east of Highway 49 by early afternoon, but that they wouldn't make it all the way to the family farm until the next day. They were down to very little in the way of food—just the few remaining energy bars he had—but he figured they could make the rest of the hike to his house on those if they had to. He wouldn't pass up an opportunity to take another rabbit or other game that presented itself, but he didn't want to go out of his way or spend a lot of extra time hunting, either.

They were able to hike all morning at a steady pace thanks to the efforts of a clearing crew that had apparently been working on this section of the right-of-way not long before the blackout. With little underbrush to contend with and a recent rutted road made by heavy equipment, they walked at full stride, slowing down only when the pipeline crossed a rural road. Most of these roads were roughly paved, but some of them were just graded gravel. Mitch told April the gravel ones were U.S. Forest Service roads, and that there were many miles of them in the national forest.

Each time they came to a road of any sort, April waited while Mitch reconnoitered ahead, since he was wearing full camouflage. It wasn't worth taking a chance of being seen if it wasn't necessary. But these remote roads were little used even in normal times, and today they crossed them without incident. It was not until they came to the highway that they saw people.

"Is that Highway 49?" April asked as they paused in a patch of high grass at the crest of a ridge, looking down at a four-lane highway that intersected the pipeline and lay in their path.

"Yes," Mitch said. "There's nothing else it could be. It's running north and south, and 49 is the only four-lane in these parts."

"How will we get across it without being seen?"

"We may not," Mitch said. He was watching the stream of people walking along the wide lanes of pavement, threading their way between stalled vehicles. It was a scene very similar to what he'd left behind in New Orleans, except this was an area well out from any large cities. It was midday Sunday, almost a week since the pulse event. He figured that by now, enough time had passed that many people, like him and April, would have had time to walk quite far, if they were motivated. And by now, many other people who probably sat tight right at first not knowing what to do, were now on the move, trying to get home, searching for their loved ones, or looking for safe refuge, food, and everything else they would need. The majority of them were headed north, but there were a few going south as well. As they watched the widely dispersed foot traffic from their vantage point, they saw an occasional bicyclist weaving through the pedestrians at a faster pace.

"Let's get closer," he said. "We need to get over in the woods, out of the right-of-way and sneak up as close to the road as we can and watch for a few minutes. Most of these people are probably harmless, but we can't be too careful. We sure don't want to try and cross in full view of some gang of thugs like those guys back on Highway 11."

ELEVEN

April crouched in the underbrush at the edge of the woods alongside Mitch. From their place of concealment, some thirty yards from the southbound lanes of the highway, they could see roughly a mile of the roadway in each direction. In this cross-section of highway, there were dozens of abandoned vehicles: cars, pickup trucks, minivans, SUVs, and eighteen-wheelers. They weren't as densely packed as on the Interstate out of New Orleans, but this was a busy highway nevertheless, connecting the Gulf Coast cities, including Gulfport and Biloxi, with Hattiesburg, Jackson, and other parts of the state to the north.

The refugees traveling the road were moving in singles, twos and threes, and occasional larger groups clustered together. They were strung out along the way as far as she and Mitch could see. Most were moving slowly, burdened by stuff they were carrying in unwieldy travel bags or luggage, some even attempting to drag large suitcases on rollers over the rough pavement. Only a few were equipped with proper backpacks, and some were pushing or pulling various wheeled load carriers, including wheelbarrows and shopping carts. The few bicyclists were threading among the walkers at an only slightly faster pace, because most of them were overloaded and riding cheap department store bikes ill-suited for long distance travel. She saw that many of the refugees had guns: rifles or shotguns carried by hand or on slings, or handguns worn in plain sight, strapped to their bodies. As they watched there was even one family of four that passed them going north on horseback, all their mounts equipped with saddlebags. The man at the lead of the group had a heavily loaded packhorse in tow, and slung over his shoulder was an assault rifle with a long magazine protruding from the receiver. He looked confident and well prepared, and the woman and two preteen boys riding close behind him appeared to be relaxed and well-acquainted with horseback travel. Where they were going, April could only guess, but she got a good look at all of them as they rode close by at a walking pace in the grass beside the highway.

The flow of human traffic paid no regard to the north or southbound lanes of the four-lane highway, and people moving in both directions used whatever lane they wanted to. There was a narrow median between the two, which was sparsely wooded in some stretches but still open enough that April and Mitch could see most of all four lanes.

"What do you think?" she whispered.

"I say we go," Mitch said. "I don't see anybody that looks too crazy. Let's wait until those folks get a little farther along, so we don't spook their horses, and then we'll go."

April followed when Mitch walked out of the woods a few moments later. He carried his bow loosely in one hand, down by his side, but there was an arrow on the string just in case he needed it. The horseback riders were now over a hundred yards away, moving north. About the same distance to the south was another group of four people, also walking north, in their direction. They appeared to be two couples traveling together, struggling under the weight of their heavy bags. They stopped immediately when Mitch stepped into the road wearing his camouflage and carrying the bow and arrow, and April didn't blame them. She waved to put their minds at ease and one of the men waved back, but they didn't start walking north again until she and Mitch were both across the median and into the northbound lanes.

As they reached the far side of the highway, Mitch paused for a moment to stare at something in the distance farther south along the road. April saw that it was a circling mass of black vultures, far more than she had ever seen concentrated in one place. They were wheeling through sky, landing and taking off from the tops of the pine trees near a tangled mass of wrecked cars. Many more were clustered in large groups on the ground, hopping around and fighting among themselves over whatever it was they had gathered to feast upon. April did not have to use much imagination to figure out what it was. "I'm sure glad we don't have to walk the highway like all these other people," she said. "It's a hopeless situation for most of them, isn't it?"

"Seems like it, I'm afraid. Come on, let's get out of here."

On the east side of the highway, unlike the section they had just traversed, the pipeline company had not cleared the right-of-way recently, and they had to push their way through underbrush and tall grass. In some places it was easier to move just inside the edge of the pine forests than out in neglected open areas, but even there they had to detour around thickets, pick their way over fallen trees and slog through deep mud. After about twenty minutes of this, April was beginning to get discouraged. At that rate it would take all afternoon

just to go two or three miles. But then they crested another small ridge and suddenly came upon a wide-open
clearing that turned out to be the right-of-way of a railroad crossing the pipeline at a perpendicular angle and
running north and south.

Mitch grinned and suggested they take a short break
to rest a bit and make a plan. "This is fantastic! How
could I have forgotten all about this railroad? I don't
know what I was thinking. That just goes to show how
much easier this would be if I just had a map."

"So what do we do now? Do we follow the railroad?"

"Yep. This has to be the railroad that goes right
through downtown Brooklyn. That's the little town
where our school is. All we have to do is follow it north
to get to Black Creek. I was thinking we would have to
find another pipeline or power line right-of-way in order to stay off the roads, but I was also afraid that looking for one would take us too far east, out of the way. We
need to go to Brooklyn first anyway, before we go to the
land, because Lisa's friend's house is right on the outskirts of town and that's where she's supposed to be."

"How far from the town is your land then?"

"Come over here, I'll show you." Mitch found a shady
spot in the edge of the woods and using his feet, kicked
away the pine straw and other debris to clear a patch
of sandy soil. Then he found a suitable stick and be-

gan roughing out a map. "It's less than ten miles, depending on how you go. Look, here's the creek." He drew a squiggly line in the sand. "Here's Highway 49, the four-lane we just crossed back there. I'm guessing only about a half mile back, considering how thick it was between here and there." Mitch drew an arrow-straight line that intersected the creek at sort of a right angle. "Highway 49 runs north and south. Brooklyn is just to the east of the highway, on the north side of the creek, right here." He scratched out a rough circle. "Our land is downstream, about here, where the county line is." He made an approximate square on the south side of the squiggly line, a good bit to the east of the highway and the circle that indicated Brooklyn. He drew another line that roughly paralleled the highway, also going through Brooklyn. "This is the railroad you're looking at. We're about here, I think." He pointed with the stick. "We need to go north to Brooklyn, and this railroad will take us there. After that, we go downstream to get to our land."

"What will we do, follow the creek?"

"No, not directly. There are too many bends and too many swampy places, not to mention the woods are too thick, even worse than what we've just come through. We can backtrack a bit on the railroad to here," he pointed again. "There's a hiking trail that runs along the south side of the creek, which is the side our land is on. The trail goes within a half mile of our house. Not many people use it anyway, and I'll bet no one is on it now."

"How long is all of this going to take? Every day that goes by is another day that something could happen to Kimberly. She could be going without food or something else she needs. It's driving me crazy."

"I know you're anxious, but it's better to get there safely than to not get there at all. At least on the railroad we can walk at night if we need to. I'm guessing it's about one o'clock right now," he said, looking at the angle of the sun. "We can get to Brooklyn sometime tonight, I'll bet, if we keep walking. If it's late when we arrive, we can camp somewhere in the woods around Black Creek and then walk to the Burns' house where Lisa is staying first thing in the morning. We'll get her and still have time to make the hike to our house tomorrow and see about getting that old truck running."

"I just hope you're right that the truck will still run, and that it'll still be there when we get there," April said.

"Don't worry about that. It'll be there, and it'll run. Hey, while we're resting for a few minutes, do you still want to try shooting my bow?"

"Sure, but what would I shoot at?"

Mitch pointed out a steep clay bank on the other side of the railroad tracks, created when the railroad bed was graded. He looked around and found a couple of discarded plastic soda bottles and walked over to the bank, fixing them in place by putting them mouth down over twigs he pushed into the clay.

"Those are small targets," April said, when he returned to her side and showed her how to hold and draw the bow.

"Yeah, but it's actually better to practice by shooting at small targets instead of large ones. It helps you focus. Archery is more mental than physical. It's all about focus and not thinking too much about the target."

"Sounds kind of like martial arts," she said.

"Well, I suppose it *is* a martial art. At least it used to be."

"And now it is again," she said. "Probably one of the more useful skills to have now, as you have already proven."

April quickly learned that Mitch's expertise just made it *look* easy. There was nothing easy about it, including simply pulling back the sixty pounds of resistance in the longbow's sturdy limbs. She could do it, but it was a bit too much weight for her to hold steadily enough to take aim, and Mitch said she would be better off starting out with a draw weight of around forty pounds until she perfected the technique. With his bow she had to shoot from a partially drawn position, and her first few arrows went completely wild, missing the mark by several yards and in no consistent pattern. When Mitch demonstrated the correct technique, easily pinning the small plastic bottles to the bank behind them with the first arrow every time April got angry at her own lackluster shots.

"It just comes with practice," he said. "You well know what I mean. You made disarming a man with a gun and smashing him where it hurts before he knew what hit him look easy, too. And you promised to teach me that, too. We'll save that for another time, though."

April knew he was right, but seeing how difficult it was made her want to master the bow even more. She was determined to do so, and Mitch said he had a lighter weight target bow at his house that she could take with her and keep, if she wanted it. When she asked how he knew so much about archery, he told her that he had read practically everything he could get his hands on about the many variations of the bow and arrow around the world. He had an encyclopedic knowledge of this weapon's development in different cultures and the role it played in shaping history. This simple piece of bent wood had been instrumental in enabling primitive hunters to dominate their environment and had later played a key role on medieval battlefields until the refinement of firearms technology. He could go on and on about it for hours, that was obvious, and April had rarely met anyone who was so passionate about anything. In this way Mitch reminded her a lot of her dad.

When they started moving again, following the railroad north, they were able to walk side-by-side again, unlike on the pipeline, and this enabled Mitch to keep talking about his favorite subject. April was interested, and wanted to know more, but she also wanted to know more about his father and his job as a game warden. Mitch told her stories that his dad had told him, about some of his encounters with poachers, marijuana growers, and other criminals who operated in the boondocks where he worked every day.

"Dad always said that being a game warden was one of the most dangerous law enforcement jobs there is. That's because practically everyone you come across out there is armed: hunters, both the legal and illegal ones, dope growers, meth heads, fugitives, you name it. He says he's been shot at more times than he can remember, but so far he's never been hit. He's one heck of a woodsman, though, and that gives him the advantage. He usually sneaks up on the bad guys and has them in the cuffs before they even know what's happening. He's kind of a legend around Perry County. Everybody up there knows who he is. He taught me just about everything I know about the woods, even if he's not much of a archer."

"I just always thought those wildlife officers and rangers did stuff like rescuing baby animals and making sure no one sets the forest on fire," said April. "It sounds like a really tough job."

The easy walking on the railroad and their conversation made the afternoon seem to go by fast, and by sunset Mitch estimated they had covered seven or eight miles since getting on the tracks and should be getting close to Brooklyn.

"Isn't it amazing? We've been walking all afternoon, and haven't seen a soul on the railroad, and look at how many people there were back on Highway 49."

"I guess they just don't know about the railroad," April said.

"Most of them probably don't. But it's also just the way people think. Most of them are still thinking like they did before the blackout. They drove cars on roads, so they think they're supposed to walk on roads. Even if they crossed right over the railroad, which I'm sure some of them did, it wouldn't occur to them to use it. It's just human nature, I guess."

When full darkness finally overtook them, neither wanted to stop, as Mitch was sure Brooklyn was within reach and April just wanted to take every step she could that would bring her closer to Kimberly. With no glow from lights to pollute the night sky, the array of stars stretching overhead above the railroad was spectacular. April had never seen such a sky living in the city, and the starlight alone was enough to see by as they walked the tracks. Two hours later, the rising moon gave them even more light, and by the time it was high above the tree tops she could see quite some distance both ahead and behind along the tracks. Sometime around midnight, when they were both getting tired and ready to stop, something ahead in the distance took shape as they approached; it was an iron bridge and April could hear the sound of running water.

"Black Creek," Mitch whispered. "We made it!"

TWELVE

Mitch kept his voice to a whisper as he warned April that they needed to slow down and approach the railroad bridge over Black Creek with caution. A paved road converged from the left and ran parallel to the railroad here, with just a few yards of open grass separating them. The road crossed the creek on a separate span upstream from the railroad bridge.

"That's Brooklyn just on the other side of those bridges," Mitch whispered. "Not much there, just a few houses, a country store, and the canoe rental place for people that come here to run the creek on summer weekends. Our school is down the road that turns off to the east at the crossroads ahead."

"Can't we walk on into the town tonight and go to your sister's friend's house and see if she's there?"

"We could, but it's probably not a good idea this late. It's after midnight, and even though I know a lot of people around here, if we go walking into town this late at night, we're liable to get shot. I'm sure everybody's on edge and anyone who sees us on the street that late will think we're strangers up to no good and probably shoot before asking questions. Let's just hole up in the woods by the creek and wait until daylight. It's only a few hours anyway."

Mitch was almost as anxious as April. It would be hard for him to wait until morning, too, but he knew it was the smart thing to do. He was looking forward to seeing Lisa and was really glad his long trek from New Orleans was almost over. As they settled into a dark grove of hardwoods near the banks of the creek, he thought about how good it was going to be to be home again sometime later that very day. On their land, he could weather this disaster until the power was eventually restored, and he would have been content but for two things: First, his parents were at best stranded hundreds of miles away and at worst could have died in plane crash. Second, his new friend, April, was still a long way from her child and he still had to somehow help her get to Hattiesburg.

Again he found himself wishing that it wasn't true that she had a daughter and a boyfriend who was the child's father. If she only had herself to worry about, none of them would have to leave the security of the land where they would have everything they needed. They could remain hidden from the rest of the world until someday when things were back to normal, and by then, maybe she wouldn't *want* to leave. But that was just a nice fantasy to keep his mind occupied and help pass the time. He knew it was impossible.

* * *

When they both finally fell asleep, it seemed like mere moments before the sunlight filtering through the oak and river birch branches overhead woke them again. Mitch walked to the edge of the creek and splashed his face. His stomach was grumbling, and he knew April had to be hungry, too. They had walked a lot of miles on too little food, but now that they had almost reached their destination, they would soon have plenty to eat. Hopefully Mrs. Burns would have groceries at her house and could offer them breakfast before they set off with Lisa to take her home. When April was ready, Mitch picked up his bow and they made their way out of the woods, up the bank to the paved road. There was no point in walking the railroad bridge across the river, as it was dangerous if someone made a misstep between the trestles, and besides, he didn't feel like they had a reason to hide any longer.

From the elevated car bridge, they could see little of the creek, as it was shrouded in early morning mist steaming off the cool water. The road into the little community had been cleared of stalled vehicles, with most of them pushed to the side or into the gravel parking lots of the store and the canoe rental place. There were a few people stirring already. A handful of older men were standing around the pumps of the one gas station in town, and another man was sitting on his front porch at a house on the other side of the street.

The man on the porch quickly got to his feet when he noticed them walking down the road. As he did, he picked up the shotgun that was leaning against the wall beside his chair and stepped down to his front lawn. Mitch had seen him around before but didn't know his name. He realized their sudden appearance first thing in the morning could be alarming. Everyone would recognize his dad at a glance, but they might not realize who Mitch was, especially in his full camo. The men at the gas station had also noticed them and were headed their way in a tight group, one carrying a rifle loosely in his hand and the others wearing pistols in plain view.

Mitch waved and held the bow up with his other hand to show that he had not drawn an arrow and was not carrying a gun. He whispered to April to wave too before he greeted the men. "Good morning, folks! It's

Mitchell Henley, Doug Henley's son!" The men were visibly relieved. They didn't want trouble, but with their town such a short distance away from Highway 49, it was inevitable that some of the refugees would be making their way there out of desperation. The people here would want to help them if they could, but there would simply be too many to allow them to stay, and they had to be wary of the few who might try taking what they wanted by force.

Mitch knew one of the men from the store well, as he often bought gas for his truck there or stopped by to get a soda. Mitch introduced April and related the story of his long walk from New Orleans, leaving out the part about the three men they'd killed but not the confiscation of April's Mustang.

"Those bastards are probably driving it right now," the man said, "using it for a patrol car since their own damned cars won't run."

"I'm sure they are, Mr. Holloway," Mitch agreed. "If Dad was around, we could drive that old Ford truck of grandpa's down there and straighten this right out. He wouldn't put up with it. I told that police chief who he was, but they claimed they never heard of him."

"Well, everyone one around *here* sure knows who Doug Henley is," Mr. Holloway said. "Especially all them damned spot lighters and dope growers out of Louisiana. You can bet they're all scared of Doug Henley, and he's been sorely missed since everything shut down last week. I sure hope he's all right, and your mother, too. They're fine folks. Like you said, if their plane had the chance to land, then your dad will be able to take care of himself and look out for your mom. I'll bet he's on his way here with her right now, and he'll get here, too, come hell or high water."

"You're probably right, I'm sure he will. But I know it could take a long time. It took long enough for us to get here just from New Orleans. I've been frantic to find my sister, Lisa. She spent the night before all this happened with her friend Stacy Burns."

Mitch knew that Mr. Holloway knew Lisa and her friend Stacy well, as Mitch sometimes had both girls with him when he stopped at the store. Stacy stayed over at the Henley's farm even more often than Lisa spent the night in Brooklyn with her. Of course, Mr. Holloway also knew Stacy's brother, Jason, and her mom, Pam Burns. In a town the size of Brooklyn, it was impossible that a storekeeper would not know every resident for miles around.

"Mitch, I'm afraid I've got to tell you that Lisa and Stacy aren't here. Neither is Jason. They left several days ago and I haven't seen 'em since."

Mitch was shocked. He had felt so sure he'd find them in town, and to find out he was wrong practically knocked the air out of his lungs.

Pam Burns was a divorced single mom, and had a good-paying job as an emergency room nurse at a hospital in Hattiesburg. Mitch knew she was going to be working the evening before he had to take his parents to the airport, and the girls would be fine going home after school with Jason until Ms. Burns got there late that evening. But according to Mr. Holloway, she never made it home:

"Jason said she called him that night when her shift was over, saying the nurse who was supposed to relieve her didn't show up. She told Jason she had agreed to stay and work a double if he could promise her he would get the girls up in the morning and to school on time. Jason told her he would, and if it hadn't been for the pulse happening that morning, she would have gotten home shortly after they left in the morning. But it did happen, and they never heard another word from her. The three of them walked down here to the store several times that first day to get something to drink and see if anybody knew what was going on.

"The next day we all figured that the power wasn't going to come back on anytime soon, so Jason, Stacy, and Lisa set out walking to your folks' place. Lisa said that old truck of your grandpa's was still sitting out there in the barn. We talked about it and figured it would still run, so Jason planned to use it to go to Hattiesburg to get his mom. I don't know what happened after that. If he did manage to get her, they didn't come back here. As far as I know, no one has been back to the Burns' house since they all left that day."

Mitch was frantic with worry now. What did this mean? Had all of them gotten in the truck and gone to Hattiesburg? Could they have gotten stuck there or broken down on the road somewhere? What if the truck had been stolen or taken from them by force? Or maybe they were safely back at the farm by now? Maybe they couldn't get the truck running and never even left? There were so many possibilities, but there was no way to get any answers until he ruled them out one by one.

"I'll bet they're all just fine and waiting out their at your folks' place," said Mr. Holloway, wary of how his news had affected Mitch. "Jason probably picked up his mom, and they decided it would be safer to stay out there than try to come back to Brooklyn, since we're so close to the main highway here."

Mitch hoped he was right but was doubtful. Wouldn't they have at least stopped back by their house to get some of their stuff? He was sure there would be things there they would need. He wanted to walk over there to check and be sure there was no sign they'd been back, just in case, but first, Mr. Holloway insisted that he and April come to his house behind the store and eat breakfast.

Mitch didn't argue with that. He was starving and April said she was, too. Bacon, fresh eggs, and biscuits were a welcome change from the spartan fare they'd had on the road. These rural folks were well set for food, at least for the foreseeable future, and with propane, wood stoves, and other essentials for living off the grid, losing the power for a while wasn't too much of a disruption in how they ate.

As April and Mitch finished their meal and last cups of coffee, April expressed her doubts about continuing on to the farm with him. "If the truck is not there anymore, I'm just going to be walking that much farther out of my way and will lose even more time getting to Kimberly," she said.

Mitch felt as if he were on the receiving end of one of her vicious kicks. "But we don't *know* that it's not there," he argued. "It's highly likely that they *did* pick up Mrs. Burns and drive back, and that it *is* there. Or it could be that Jason and the girls couldn't figure out how to get it running anyway. Jason doesn't know anything about mechanics, as far as I know. If any of them could get it going, it would be Lisa, but who knows?"

"That's the problem," April said. "We just don't know. I'm thinking I should just try to make my way to Hattiesburg from here, while I'm closer."

"That would be crazy!" Mitch said, starting to panic at the thought of them suddenly parting. "You know by now how dangerous it is to travel at all, much less *alone*. We need to stick together, like we planned."

"I don't want to go alone, but I know you can't go with me. Your first responsibility is your sister, and I wouldn't expect you not to look for her first."

"Then just go with me to my house. It won't take long. I'll find her and then I promise you I'll help you get to Hattiesburg, one way or the other. I won't let you down."

When they left Mrs. Holloway's kitchen, April still wasn't sure. He managed to talk her into walking with him the short distance to the Burns' house. After looking around the outside and peering in the windows and doors, it appeared that no one had been there for a while.

"Wherever they are, it looks like they didn't come back here after they left. Look, April, it will only take a few hours to get to my house and find out if the truck is there or not. If it is, it could make all the difference. If you go on alone from here, *anything* could happen. Will you at least take a chance that it's there?"

"I'll go with you today, but if it's not there, I can't wait any longer and with or without the truck, and with or without you, I'm heading straight for Hattiesburg."

"Okay, that's a deal. Either way, you won't regret it. If you do have go on alone, at least you'll be even better armed than you are now. I'll make sure of that."

They walked back to Mr. Holloway's store on the way back to the intersection of the road and the hiking trail. "It'll take you most of the day to walk home on that trail, Mitch," the store owner said. "You know that last big storm we had knocked down a lot of trees over the path, and the forest service hasn't cleared them all out yet. Why don't y'all just run the creek? Heck, with the way it's been raining, it's up a lot. I'll bet you can get there in five or six hours on that current."

"I would, but my canoe is at the house, so that kind of defeats the purpose, and I doubt the canoe rental place is open this week," Mitch said with a laugh.

"That ain't a problem at all, Mitch. The outfitter left, that's true. He had that old diesel Landcruiser that he kept around back, so he was going somewhere over in Louisiana where his wife was from. But he left me a key to the building and his storage yard. I know he won't mind if Doug Henley's son borrows one of his canoes. Your dad has helped him out a bunch of times when he's had boats stolen and that time somebody broke in his cabin."

"Wow, that would be great! A canoe *would* get us there a lot faster. Have you ever been canoeing, April?"

"No, but I'll learn quick if it means it gets us there faster," she said.

THIRTEEN

Mitch seemed almost elated as they shoved off from the sandbar under the bridge in an aluminum rental canoe, a ticket back to his home that would be so much easier than walking. But April knew that every positive thought he had must have been dampened by concern for Lisa. All this time, he had been sure that she was safe at the Burns' house, but now she could be out on the road somewhere—the same treacherous road that the two of them had just come from. Lisa could be in real and immediate danger. Anything could have happened if she'd attempted that trip with Jason and Stacy in the old truck, and Mitch was sure that she would have gone with them, as they would not have left her there alone.

Mitch dug his paddle in with strong strokes, determined to get home as fast as possible, and April did her best to help him. Although she had never been in a canoe before, she picked up the paddling technique quickly after Mitch gave her a few pointers. From her position in the bow, all she really had to do was provide extra power, while he maneuvered the slender, seventeen-foot craft through the logjams, snags, and gravel shoals of the stream. Running the creek in the silent canoe, Mitch said he felt much more at ease than on any part of the route they had taken so far, including the isolated pipeline. Black Creek flowed for dozens of miles through remote national forestlands, and aside from a few access points, it was far removed from roads. They rounded bend after bend, seeing no signs of people but lots of wildlife, including herons, kingfishers, wood ducks, and at one point even a deer drinking from the edge of the water.

April couldn't help but notice the beauty of her surroundings: mile after mile of magnificent old pines and hardwoods and the clear, whiskey-colored waters of the swift-running creek that swept their canoe past contrasting white sandbars like a magic carpet.

"This is an incredible place," April said, looking around her as they slipped beneath high clay banks topped with towering pines that seemed to rake the sky above.

"It is that," Mitch said. "Most of our land looks just like this, except our creek isn't big enough to canoe."

"I can see why you said it was a good place to be after what's happened. I can't imagine the refugees finding their way here anytime soon."

"We can hope not," Mitch said.

Though the natural beauty awed her, she almost felt
guilty for enjoying it. Here she was on the fourth day
after leaving New Orleans, still not in Hattiesburg with
her child, and at the moment traveling in the wrong
direction to get there. She trusted that Mitch was doing the best he could to help her, but there had been so
many setbacks. None of them were his fault, but even
so, she had to remind herself that she was not his prior-
ity, despite the bond that had developed between them
because of what they'd been through in their short time
together.

With Mitch's sister missing, April knew that he
would not stop until he did everything in his power to
find her. On top of that, if the old truck was gone, April's
hope of an easier way to get to Hattiesburg was gone
with it. She would still have to walk, and as they skated
quickly on the current she wondered if she had made a
mistake getting in the canoe with Mitch.

Even if the truck was still there, it might be more
dangerous to try and drive it than it would be to continue walking. There could be more roadblocks, more
crooked cops, or more men like the three on Highway

11. After Mitch opened her eyes to alternative routes like pipelines and railroads, she knew that if she *did* have to walk, it would not be on the main roads. If she had parted ways with him that morning, she could have just continued north on the railroad that ran through Brooklyn. But she had to admit she didn't like the idea of going alone, even on that route.

As Mitch had pointed out, despite her martial arts skills, the only weapon she had was her knife, and being alone would put her at a disadvantage in a confrontation, especially if there were more than one person involved. And while she was fascinated with the bow and arrow after seeing his skill with it, and was determined to master it herself someday, even if she had one of her own, it wouldn't do her much good given her current skill level. What she needed was a gun, and Mitch promised her that once they got to his house she would have one. Between him and his father, they had a variety of firearms to choose from, and when she and Mitch parted, he would make sure she was well-armed so she could protect herself and her family.

That alone was worth the extra time it would take to make the side trip to his land, even if she did end up having to go alone from there to Hattiesburg. From what she had seen, things were not going to get better anytime soon. Wherever she ended up with Kimberly,

David, and his parents, there would likely be more threats to deal with.

David didn't have a firearm of any kind because owning one would violate the terms of his probation. Before she had met him, he got caught selling a small amount of marijuana, but he had stayed out of trouble since and certainly didn't want to risk going to jail. She didn't know if his dad had one in their house or not, but she didn't recall any mention of it if he did.

She could only speculate as to what the conditions might be in a small city like Hattiesburg. As Mitch said, it was not big enough to be as desperate as New Orleans, but even so, 50,000 people was no small number. Unlike in rural communities like Brooklyn, most of those people would not be equipped to continue the day-to-day necessities of living without electricity, grocery stores, and cars. Mitch said that Hattiesburg was hit hard by Hurricane Katrina, and the grid had been down there for an extended time, but outside help had quickly flooded into the region after the storm had passed. Shelters were opened and basic needs were provided for. Without that help from the outside, the situation there now was bound to be vastly different.

Mr. Holloway and the other men in Brooklyn hadn't had any more news than the other people she and Mitch had met—just rumors spread from some of the refugees passing through. It seemed that no one knew anyone who had been in contact with a place that was not affected by the blackout. Even with a few older vehicles still running, no one they talked to came from anywhere beyond the scope of the event. Every day they kept hoping information would find its way there, but so far like everyone else, they were still in the dark in more ways than one.

As they paddled down the creek, April kept expecting some change in the scenery around each bend, an open field perhaps, or a house or some other sign of humanity. Yet mile after mile, the stream wound through seemingly endless forest, broken only by a single bridge they passed beneath, which Mitch said was a little-used county road. It felt as though they were in a trackless wilderness, and the total absence of sounds from manmade machinery, even from distant roads or passing planes, added to that effect. Mitch told her that in reality, despite the feeling of isolation among the tall trees, they were not that far from paved roads that roughly paralleled Black Creek's course. If they were to set out walking at right angles to the creek, they could find a road within a mile or so on either side.

"I sometimes wish that weren't the case, but the reality is that there are roads everywhere in this state and everywhere else in the country really, except in a few big areas out West like that place in Montana I told you about, where Dad took me hunting."

"Well, it sure seems like a wilderness here to me," April said. "I guess those roads don't mean much anymore if no one has a vehicle to drive on them."

"True. It does make a place like this much more inaccessible, kind of like it used to be in the old days. Given what's happened, that's a good thing, and that's why I am so grateful for our land down here. I've been thinking about how all this is going to play out and wondering just how many people living in the cities and bigger towns are going to actually make their way out of the crowds and to the country. I mean, I don't know much about cities, maybe you can correct me if I'm wrong, but wouldn't you think that most people there would know that if there is nothing left to eat in the stores, their only hope is out in the country, where the farms are?"

"Sure, I think so. Everybody knows their food comes from farms, but I haven't seen much to eat so far on this whole journey. So where *are* all the farms out here?"

"Unfortunately, there are not many at all left in south Mississippi. People that own land around here grow pine trees, not food crops. There's more money in it, and it doesn't require much work. A lot of the landowners live somewhere else anyway. It's not like it was in my grandpa's day. He was always telling me how they raised everything they ate. They grew vegetables, ground their own cornmeal, made their own cane sugar, slaughtered their own chickens and hogs. They were *completely* self-sufficient. There aren't many people living that way nowadays, even way out here.

"There are a few small cattle operations, but most are like my dad's, just a part-time hobby. Some people still grow corn or watermelons, or maybe soybeans, and of course a lot of country folk keep up a small garden around the house, but no one I know of lives completely off of their land the way they did in Grandpa's day. So I guess even if some of those people make it out of the cities, they are going to be disappointed in what they find. That's what really worries me. When they get desperate enough, *hungry* enough, there's just no telling what people will do—even good people—not to mention the kind like those three who murdered that poor old couple."

"It's really scary," April agreed. "It could turn into something like a war, I guess, with everybody fighting over food and whatever medicine is still left."

"It could even be worse than a war," Mitch said, "because practically *everybody* will be involved in it, not just soldiers like in a conventional war. Even people who don't want to fight will have to fight to defend themselves and their property and supplies, if they have any."

"Speaking of soldiers, where are they anyway? Why haven't we seen any sign of the military? They help out after hurricanes and other disasters. Where are they now?"

"You can bet that they're busy wherever they are," Mitch said, "and I'll bet they're involved in maintaining order in a lot of places, they're just probably not operating far from their bases. But as a matter of fact, there's a major Army National Guard base not far to the north of here. It's called Camp Shelby. It's a major training area for the Guard and regular soldiers heading for overseas combat. They've even built simulated Iraqi and Afghan villages there for training purposes. Sometimes we can hear artillery and heavy machine gun fire from our land on the weekends when they're doing a lot of training.

"They also use parts of the national forest for special exercises. I'm sure the entire place is locked down under tight security right now, so that's probably another thing we should be aware of. The base covers a large area, and it's pretty much between our place and Hattiesburg. Some of the back roads I know to get to Hattiesburg either go through part of it or pass close to it."

"Are there other ways to get there? The last thing I want to do is go through another roadblock."

"Oh yeah, there are *lots* of back roads going everywhere, and I know most of the ones north of here a lot better than the area we walked through. It might involve a roundabout route, but there are alternatives to going near the base or getting on the main highways."

April paddled on in silence. Another obstacle between her and Hattiesburg was the last thing she needed. Mitch always seemed to have an answer to every problem that came up, or at least he *said* he did. At least the canoeing *was* easier than walking, and seemed to be faster, too, judging by how the trees on the bank slipped past them. She had no way of estimating distance out here, though—everything looked the same. The hours were passing along, though, that was easy to tell as the sun finally climbed high enough that the streamside trees didn't shade the river fully, and the morning cool changed to almost uncomfortable warmth. She could feel the sun on her exposed arms and face and though she knew it might give her sunburn if she were out here long enough, it was much better than walking in the drenching rain.

They paddled without stopping through the morning, still full of energy from the hearty breakfast at the Holloways' house. It was the first time they'd been well fed since losing the car, and April trusted there would be plenty of food at Mitch's house after he had told her how his mom kept the pantry stocked. Again she started to feel guilty—she was going to have plenty while her Kimberly might be doing without. It was a struggle to push those thoughts out of her mind, but April knew she had to take care of herself if she wanted to maintain the strength to get back to her baby and look out for her.

As they rounded a bend, Mitch snapped her out of her thoughts by announcing, "We're almost there! Just past that sandbar ahead, that's where we get off the river. I know a shortcut that will take us right to our land."

"What are we going to do with the canoe, leave it on the bank?" April asked as they paddled past a sandbar and Mitch steered them into an eddy that lay behind it.

"No, someone might find it. We've got a couple of canoes at the house, but with this situation being what it is, you never know what will happen. I may need it later, or if I don't, someone I know might. We don't have to carry it far, but I'd like to haul it at least a couple hundred yards up into the woods and hide it. That way I'll know where it is even if I don't need it, and when all this mess gets straightened out, I can return it to the rental people it belongs to."

Mitch ran the bow up onto the sand and April stepped out of the boat. Then he hopped out and put both of their paddles inside. It took both their strength to drag the canoe up the bank, and then they carried it between them, Mitch at the bow, leading the way. When they were a good distance from the creek, he led the way into a thicket of dense evergreen shrubs that he said were bay trees. It was the perfect place to hide something as big as a canoe. After covering the overturned hull with branches and leaf litter from the forest floor, it was invisible to anyone who might happen to walk through the area along the creek bank. This done, they shouldered their light bags again and set off on foot, Mitch leading the way with growing anticipation.

April followed him along an unseen path that led through an expansive area of huge old-growth hardwoods with a canopy so dense they were walking in the shade most of the time. Then the terrain turned hilly, and the hardwoods gave way to more pines, similar to the forests they had traversed along the pipeline, but with taller trees. Other than their own footsteps, the only sounds were birdsongs and hammering noises that Mitch said were made by big pileated woodpeckers. The forest here was beautiful, much different than the scrubby, under-brushed choked woods they had passed through on most of their journey. April could see why Mitch talked about his land so much, and as they walked, they crossed some invisible boundary she would have never guessed was there and he announced that they were now entering the six hundred acres of the Henley family property.

FOURTEEN

The route from the banks of Black Creek through the forest to the Henley property boundary was intentionally obscure. Black Creek, being a federally designated national wild and scenic river and flowing mostly through public forestlands, was a popular destination for canoeing. In the peak summer season, it attracted hordes of recreational paddlers, especially on weekends. Most of the paddlers kept to the river and seldom ventured far into the surrounding woods, but hunters and fishermen with small, outboard-powered John boats used the creek, too, as a travel corridor to access remote areas away from roads where there was less competition for their quarry. Many of the deer hunters motored far upstream and pulled their boats up to the bank at a likely spot to hunt the bottomland forests in the vicinity.

Any kind of well-marked path or track would be an open invitation to follow it, so Mitch's dad had always cautioned him to avoid making obvious trails from the creek to their property line by taking care to avoid using the same route too often. Having traveled so many different ways, Mitch knew the national forestlands in the area where they landed the canoe like the back of his hand. He didn't need trails or markers, because he was familiar with the lay of the land, even though he knew to a stranger like April, it would all look the same.

Mitch had long since learned that when navigating dense forests areas like this, it was impossible to get lost if you followed the drainages, both the tiny tributaries that fed the larger creek and the dry draws in the hollows between subtle ridges. To Mitch these were as obvious as city streets, and he knew every one of them within miles of his house. Such natural corridors could be easily overlooked by someone unfamiliar with them, and people who got lost here often pushed through the thickets and up and down the hills and hollows, trying to walk in a straight line but invariably getting off course before they made it far. Mitch had encountered lost hunters and hikers in these woods on more than one occasion and lead them back to where they'd lost their way.

Given the current situation, it was likely some of the traveling refugees would eventually make their way here, but he doubted anyone would find their way to his place from the creek. More likely they would come by way of the county road, finding the house if they ventured down the long gravel lane leading to it. That was the only entrance to the property other than this backdoor route from the creek. Mitch had already been thinking about what he could do to secure that entrance once he got home and made sure Lisa was there, too. He wished he could simply hide it somehow, but that would be virtually impossible. He could at least fell a couple of large trees across the lane and render it impassible by car, but anyone approaching on foot could go around such a roadblock. A barbed wire fence enclosed the part of the property adjacent to the road to keep the thirty or so head of cattle on the two forties out front, but such a fence was no obstacle to a human.

Like Mark Rainey, the landowner who'd surprised them by their campfire near the pipeline, Mitch knew he was going to have to make regular patrols of the property part of his routine until things got back to normal. It was not that he would mind if someone passing through needed to camp on their land for the night. That was fine, and he would help them if he could. Far more worrying, though, was the idea of the truly desperate coming to the house and trying to take what they had there or poaching the cattle that would be much easier prey than wild game like deer. Mitch knew he was going to have his hands full, but first he had to make sure Lisa was okay and then figure out what to do about April.

The transition from national forestland into the Henley property was not marked by a fence or even a posted sign. The cattle were acres away on the other side of property, and the lower sections closest to the creek were still in a natural state of mature pines mixed with a few hardwoods. Mitch knew where the line was because it paralleled a slight elevation change that put it right on the edge of the creek's flood plain. As he crossed that invisible line, he felt a great sense of well being, at least for his own security, and he tried to remain positive about the odds of finding Lisa at home as he quickened his steps in the direction of the house.

"I can't believe you live out here," April whispered as she followed close behind. "There's nothing but woods!"

Mitch laughed a little and told her that the house wasn't exactly *in* the woods. They did have pasturelands on their acreage, too. "We even have a yard," he said, "with azaleas and rose bushes and hedges and grass I have to mow in the summertime—just like people in the suburbs. You'll see."

As if to prove his point, they reached the edge of the first pasture just minutes later. Mitch wanted to be cautious about approaching the house, though, just in case someone was there who was not supposed to be. That was easy, because when he started bow-hunting years before he had made a series of trails around the edges of the fields, just inside the trees, where he could move without being seen. The hidden routes came in handy for stalking rabbits and grazing deer, allowing him to move silently and unnoticed.

The path around this first pasture led up a gradual slope. At the top a narrow band of trees separated it from another field where his grandfather used to keep horses. Mitch had a path within that buffer zone of trees as well, and he led April along it until they emerged in a clearing behind an old wooden barn.

"That's where Dad keeps that old tractor I told you about," Mitch whispered.

He led her along the back side of the barn and then motioned for her to wait while he crept forward to the far corner to have a look at the house. From this vantage point he could see the back of the house without being seen, and he crouched there, looking and listening for any sign that Lisa or anyone else might be there. But it was quiet and nothing was moving except for a few of the cows he could see grazing in the pasture on the other side of the yard.

From this angle, Mitch could not see into the carport to tell whether or not his mom's car or the antique Ford truck was still in there. He could, however, see that his dad's dark green patrol truck, furnished by the Mississippi Department of Wildlife, Fisheries, and Parks, was parked where it always was, next to a shed on the side of the house where his state-provided patrol boat was also sitting on its trailer. Mitch had expected the state truck to be there. It was a Chevrolet Sierra 4x4 only a year older than his dad's brand-new personal truck and certainly wouldn't run after the pulse.

What he did not expect to see, though, was that the driver's side window of the pickup was shattered. Someone must have deliberately broken it. Lisa did not know where the spare hidden key to the vehicle was because of the rifle his father kept locked in its special security rack inside the truck, but he had been entrusted with knowledge of both the truck key and the weapon lock. The rifle was his father's state-issued Smith&Wesson M&P 15, a semi-automatic 5.56mm carbine with standard thirty-round capacity magazines. It stayed in the truck all the time, secured in special locking rack that held it in an upright position right beside the driver's seat.

Mitch wondered if Lisa and her friends would have broken into the truck to get the rifle, given the circumstances. It was not out of the question, because all of the other firearms he and his dad owned were locked in a gun safe that would have been much harder to get into. It was not that Lisa didn't know how to use them, but their dad just didn't think she was old enough to be entrusted with access to them, especially since she often had friends from school over and they might not have the same respect for firearms that he had ingrained in the two of them since they were old enough to handle BB guns.

Mitch didn't doubt for a minute that Stacy Burns' brother, Jason, would break into the truck to get that rifle. Mitch didn't particularly like him, but on the other hand, if the three of them *did* try to go to Hattiesburg to get their mom, they needed to be armed and he hoped they were. Lisa would have probably told him it was okay to do it, because she was smart enough to know it would be too dangerous to travel unarmed if there was any possible alternative.

But crouching there at the corner of the barn, Mitch had no way of knowing for sure who had broken into the truck. Could it have been someone else who got to the house first? Could they still be around, maybe even inside the house now? That was certainly a possibility, and he couldn't afford to be careless. He crept back to April's side and whispered to her, explaining the situation. He asked her to stay put and keep quiet while he made his way around to the other side of the house where he could get a view of the front entrance while staying out of sight.

Drawing an arrow and nocking it on the string, just in case, he set out to skirt the perimeter of the yard, slipping from one clump of bushes to the next, following a route he had memorized as a kid when he had practiced sneaking up on family members in his endless games of pretending to be an Apache scout or a wily mountain man. It was through those games that he'd developed the stalking skills that served him so well as a hunter now, and he was confident in his ability to move around the house undetected by anyone who might be inside, especially wearing full camouflage as he was today.

Taking no chances, he moved slowly, stopping often to look and listen until he reached a point that allowed him to see into the carport. What he saw when he did was exactly what he had feared he would find; the old Ford truck was *gone!* His mom's Trailblazer was still there, right where she always parked it, and from where he stood he couldn't see any sign that it had been broken into. The side door into the house from the carport and the main front door appeared to be intact, too.

Mitch felt it was reasonable to assume that if someone other than his sister and her friends had been there and broken into his dad's truck and taken the old one, they would have also broken into the house to see what they could find. Still, he was almost certain that Lisa, Stacy, and Jason were who had been here, and they had taken the truck. He cursed under his breath. If only he had gotten here sooner—and he would have if only those stupid cops hadn't taken April's Mustang. Now there was no telling what kind of danger his sister and her friends could be facing, and he was stuck here without transportation and unsure what to do about looking for them. On top of all that, he now had to tell April the bad news that she wasn't going to get a ride to Hattiesburg.

After several minutes of watching to make sure the house was empty, Mitch crossed the lawn to the carport and retrieved the hidden key from under a rock in one of his mom's flower beds. The door was locked as it should have been, and there was no sign it had been damaged or forced open. There was also no note on the door for him, which really made him curse under his breath. Lisa should have known that he would make his way straight back to the house as soon as possible. She could have at least let him in on her plan with a note. Then he realized that maybe she left it inside on the kitchen table instead. He unlocked the deadbolt and stepped inside, almost choking on the smell of death that greeted him in the kitchen. Mitch covered his mouth and nose with one hand as he fought back the urge to vomit and the sudden feeling of panic at what he might discover.

When he recovered, it only took a moment to realize the source of the smell. The power had been off for over a week. The refrigerator and the extra freezer in the pantry had thawed out in the warm spring weather and, of course, the fifty or sixty pounds of venison and beef stored in them had begun to rot. The kitchen floor was a sticky mess from the ice cream and frozen foods that had melted and leaked out of the smaller freezer in the top of the refrigerator unit. Mitch cursed again. *Why didn't Lisa get Stacy and Jason to help her throw all that thawing meat out before they left?* Maybe the smell wasn't so bad when they were here or maybe it didn't occur to them, but now the house was uninhabitable until something was done about it. He couldn't stand it for long, but he made a quick trip down the hall to check Lisa's bedroom and the gun safe in his dad's office. Her closet doors were open and some of her dresser drawers were half open, as if she had hurriedly rummaged through them to grab a few things and go. But when he checked the safe, he was relieved to see that it was still undisturbed. He opened the combination lock and grabbed his Ruger .357 Magnum revolver that he had stashed there right before they left for the airport. The Ruger was in its leather holster with a belt already threaded through it, lying right beside his dad's Glock 22 .40 caliber service pistol. Mitch left the Glock there and strapped the Ruger on outside his shirt before locking the safe and heading back out to the barn to get April. He dreaded telling her about the truck, and as he rounded the corner to her hiding place his anxiety doubled at the anticipation in her eyes.

"They're not here," he said. "Neither is the old truck. It looks like they were here briefly and just as I was afraid they would, they must have taken it to go look for Stacy and Jason's mother. They also broke into my dad's truck and got his patrol rifle."

April recoiled as if she'd been hit. Her hopes of a ride to Hattiesburg were gone with the truck, and Mitch could see what was going through her mind—that she'd followed him here for nothing. "How do you know it was them?" she asked. "I mean, maybe someone else took it?"

"I wondered about that, too, at first," he said, "but no, it was them. The house wasn't broken into, and I could tell Lisa went in her room and got some clothes and things. They must not have been here long at all. Just long enough to get the truck running and get dad's rifle. I don't blame them for taking the rifle, and I'm glad they have it, but I wish they'd taken a few minutes bag up the thawed-out food in the freezer and get it out of the house. I've got to warn you, the smell of rotting meat in that house will make you puke."

"I see you have a gun," April said. "Is that the only one they didn't take?"

"No, this is just my everyday around-the-farm carry gun, the one I told you I should've had with me when I got stuck in New Orleans. We've got lots more guns, you can be sure of that, and like I promised, I'm going to fix you up so that hopefully you won't have use that knife again. But it looks like you're not going to have to worry about going to Hattiesburg alone anyway. I have no way of knowing if they're still there or where they are by now, but since they're not here, there's no reason I have to be, either."

FIFTEEN

April followed Mitch as he led her from the barn to the house, first stopping by the dark green truck to see just what was missing. "I knew it was the rifle they were after," Mitch said. "It looks like Lisa or Jason must have found Dad's hacksaw in the tool shed and cut right through the locking rack. That AR-15 wouldn't be my first choice, but I'm glad they've got it if they did try to go to Hattiesburg. They sure needed *something.* I know Dad had several loaded thirty-round magazines in here, too, and it looks like they found them."

"Well, I like ARs," April said. "Dad taught me to shoot his Bushmaster, and I could hit with it better than anything else I tried." April couldn't help but notice the look of surprise on Mitch's face. "I *told* you I knew a little about guns," she explained.

"I know, I guess you did. I just figured you meant a little plinking with .22 rifles or something. But, yeah, the AR is an accurate rifle, or at least the good ones can be. But around here in these woods, you don't always get a long shot. Dad wasn't especially fond of the Smith&Wesson M&P 15 the department issued him, but he had no choice in the matter. All the wildlife officers used to carry riot-style shotguns for anything their pistols wouldn't handle: Remington Model 870 pumps in 12-gauge, 3-inch Magnum. Dad always said if he was approaching a truckload of out-of-state poachers at two o'clock in the morning, he didn't want to have to think about aiming if they all of a sudden piled out of the cab and started shooting. That's where that short pump shotgun comes into its own. You can clear an entire road with it in short order. He petitioned for the right to keep his in addition to the AR, and the department agreed, as long as he qualified with it on a regular basis. So he rarely took the AR out of the rack."

"So where is the shotgun? Do you think your sister and her friends took it, too?"

"Nope. I'm willing to bet it's locked in that toolbox in back right now. Dad kept it there out of sight when he wasn't on duty. When he was working a call where he thought he might need it, it was on the passenger's seat right beside him. Lisa didn't know where the spare truck keys were, that's why they broke out the window. I do and I'm going back in the house to get them right now. Then, I'm going to get that horrid meat out of the house so the smell won't knock you down when you come in."

"What are we going to do then? We're not going to waste time here, are we?"

"No, but there are things we need. Food for one: I mean non-perishables other than what was in the refrigerator and freezers, of course. I don't know what Lisa and her friends took but I doubt they got everything. I've got some other gear I need to get together, too, and the other weapons we'll need. Then there are Dad's topo maps. We're sure going to need them."

"So I guess we're back to walking, huh? How long is that going to take?"

"No, we're not walking. We're going to take a boat ride."

"A boat ride? Back up that creek we just came down?" April looked at the large, flat green aluminum patrol boat sitting on its trailer under the shed. A massive-looking, black outboard motor was mounted on the stern, and the telltale blue lights on elevated poles identified it as a law enforcement boat. "That thing will never run after the pulse."

"No," Mitch sighed. "That Johnson 115 is too big for Black Creek anyway. And Black Creek won't take us to

Hattiesburg, but the Leaf River will. That's the river Dad uses this boat on."

"Well, if it won't run, then how is it going to do us any good, and how would we get it to another river even if it did run? How far away is the Leaf River from here?"

"One thing at a time," Mitch said. "Let me go get that toolbox key so I can get the shotgun out. I'll feel better having it handy. You never know who may come down the road out there and figure out the lane leads to a house. I'll be right back, okay?"

While she waited outside, April looked around the neatly landscaped yard surrounding the Henley family home. It could have been an average middle-class home in suburbia but for the fact that there was no paved street out front, no adjoining lawns nor any sign of a neighboring house in the vicinity. Where the close-cropped grass of the yard ended, a barbed wire fence separated the family's living area from the domain of the small herd of brown and white cows that grazed in the pasture beyond. The gravel lane that was the only access to the house from the road was shaded by rows of tall pecan trees, their branches intertwining overhead to make the driveway almost tunnel-like. Beyond the pasture in the distance, a wall of evergreen pines marked the transition to more surrounding forest. It was an idyllic setting, but April couldn't imagine living in such isolation from other people, even with the power working and cell phone and Internet access providing a connection to the rest of the world. The house seemed so far removed from anything else, she had a hard time picturing any refugees finding their way here, but Mitch was sure they eventually would.

She looked regretfully at the empty spot in the double carport where Mitch said the old Ford truck should have been parked. It was just one more disappointment and setback keeping her from Kimberly, but like every other time this had happened, Mitch claimed to have an answer. She didn't know why she continued to trust him, but she had to admit she did feel safer in his company, and while things hadn't worked out like she'd hoped, none of it had been his fault. He was doing the best he could to help her and to find his sister. Still, it puzzled her how they were going to get there in a boat. Paddling the canoe down Black Creek had been relatively easy, but they had only gone a few miles, and Hattiesburg had to be much farther if they went by water. It would take a long time to cover so much distance that way, even with the help of the current, and she had no idea whether they would be going upstream or down Leaf River.

When he finally came back out of the house, he was carrying two long guns in addition to the revolver he'd already been wearing from his first trip inside. "I got these out of the safe," he said. "This old bolt-action Marlin .22 is my favorite all-around hunting rifle. I've had it since I was nine years old. It will be useful to keep us well fed, though I still plan to use the bow as much as possible because it's quieter. And it's not an AR, but this Ruger Mini 14 is chambered for the same caliber and has thirty-round magazines. I thought you might like it, since you said you're familiar with ARs. It's not quite as accurate, but it's still good enough at the kind of ranges you're likely to need it for. I've got the truck keys, so we'll have Dad's shotgun, and there are several pistols in the safe that I'll show you later so you can pick out what you like.

"Meanwhile, you can keep the Ruger with you. It's got a great sling, and it's short and handy to carry. There's no point in being caught off guard from now on. The next time we run into trouble, we'll be ready."

April took the short carbine Mitch held out to her. It was compact and felt solid with its dark walnut stock and machined stainless steel receiver. The combination of the straight wooden stock and extended, military-looking black magazine protruding from the receiver gave it the look of a strange hybrid, part hunting rifle and part assault weapon. She opened the bolt halfway to check that the chamber was empty, exposing the double-stacked 5.56mm steel-jacketed rounds that were loaded and waiting to be fed from the magazine as fast as she could pull the trigger.

April had loved shooting semi-automatic rifles with her dad, burning up ammo at an alarming rate, at least as much as he would allow her. But the last time they had gone shooting together was nearly four years ago. Thinking of that almost brought tears to her eyes as she slowly closed the bolt and slung the Ruger on her shoulder. She was grateful for what he taught her and knew he would be proud of how she'd handled herself in this crisis so far. He would be glad that at last she was properly armed to deal with whatever may lie in store, though she doubted he would have ever imagined her having to face a world as dangerous as hers had suddenly become.

Mitch climbed up into the truck bed and opened the toolbox while she was examining the rifle. "It's still here," he said, holding up an all-black shotgun, which, like the Ruger carbine, was short and fitted with a basic straight stock. The big difference, though, was the massive size of the barrel and the extended tubular magazine that ran full length along the underside of it. "You might not like shooting this one so much. It kicks like a mule, but it can sure sling a lot of lead in a hurry!"

"You keep it then. I'm happy with the carbine. It feels good and I'll bet I can hit with it."

"You can try it if you like before we get going. There's no shortage of places to shoot around here. I don't reckon I need to show you how."

"Nope. It's not much different than the Bushmaster Dad had. No need for lessons with this, but sometime later I still want to try the bow again."

"I've got a bow in the house for you, too. I haven't forgotten about that. Hey, you still owe me a lesson in that Kenpo stuff, too."

"I know. But first, you want to tell me how we're supposed to get to Hattiesburg by boat?"

"Of course. That's what I was just about to show you." Mitch hopped down out of the truck bed and opened the driver's side door, the one with the smashed window. He emerged with a large book he pulled from behind the seat, and opened it, taking out a stack of folded maps from between the pages. "This is a topo atlas of the entire state," he said, laying out the book on the hood of the truck, where he flipped through it to the page he was looking for. "Those folded maps are more detailed, and we'll use them to navigate, but look at this: The smaller-scale maps in the atlas show the rivers pretty well."

April leaned over the hood beside him, watching as he pointed out the location of the Henley property, the city of Hattiesburg, and the Leaf River. The squiggly blue line representing this river was much larger than the one indicating Black Creek. The Leaf River did indeed run right by Hattiesburg, just to the east of it, close to what he said was the old downtown area, but at no point did it pass near the Henley farm. Instead it ran well to the north of Black Creek, almost parallel to it, both of them curving gradually southeast and eventually merging into the much larger Pascagoula River closer to the coast. "How will that help us? It looks to me like that river's a long way from here." April used her fingers to roughly measure the distance with the aid of the mileage scale in the corner of the map. "Isn't that about fifteen miles? How could we carry a boat that far? It's too far to even carry the canoe."

"Not really. The voyageurs back in the fur trade days used to carry canoes on portages much farther than that, just like the Indians that showed them how did it for no telling how long before they showed up."

"Yeah, but we're not voyageurs . . . or Indians. For the amount of effort it would take to carry a canoe that far, wouldn't it be easier just to walk all the way to Hattiesburg?"

"If we didn't have anything to carry, yes. But we're going to be well equipped this time: the guns, lots of food, camping gear, extra clothes . . . way too much to carry all the way on foot. And besides, going by river will keep us off the roads and away from most of the problems. The Leaf River runs through woods the whole way, just like Black Creek. Once we get closer to the city, that's going to be a lot more critical. I know the back roads between here and the Leaf, at least to the closest point that it passes to here. We can get there mostly on gravel roads and probably won't come in contact with many people on the way."

"So what do we do when we get there?" April asked. "It looks like a long way to Hattiesburg going around all those bends. How long will it take us to paddle there?"

"We're not going to paddle. It would take way too long because we're going to be going upstream. We could do it if we *had* to, but I don't think we're going to have to. Come on, let's go back to the barn and I'll show you."

April wondered what new surprise Mitch had up his sleeve now. The barn was closed from the front with heavy double gates of rough sawn boards hung on massive iron hinges and secured with a big chain and padlock. Mitch had the key to the lock on the same ring as the key to his dad's truck toolbox, and he opened it and unfastened the chains, swinging back one gate, then the other. The first thing she saw inside was a red tractor, its paint faded and dull wherever its metal surfaces were not covered in rust.

"My grandpa's old tractor," Mitch explained. "It doesn't look like much, but it still runs just fine. These old Internationals are great."

"Is your grandpa still living?" April asked.

"No, he passed away when I was eleven. He was eighty four. My grandma had died the year before, and I think he was just tired of living without her. Anyway, there's nothing on this old diesel engine that would have been affected by the electromagnetic pulse. It ought to run just fine. We used it for bush-hogging mainly. But it can do a lot of things—like pull a boat!"

April looked where Mitch was pointing and saw a smaller version of the blunt-ended flat-bottomed patrol boat that was parked outside by his dad's truck. This one was also flat green, but lacked the department markings of the state-issued boat. It was on a much smaller trailer, and April noticed that the tires were almost flat. There was no engine on the back of this one, and nothing inside but bare metal seats and some old fishing poles.

"I know what you're thinking," Mitch said. "But this boat is a lot lighter weight than Dad's state boat. He uses it sometimes when he's working on Black Creek and needs to go upstream. It's only fourteen feet long, so it can get in some tight places, and it doesn't take much to push it." He walked around the boat to the barn wall on the other side and pulled a dusty feed sack off of something leaning there. April saw that it was a boat motor.

"Will that run?" she asked, doubtfully.

"I don't see why not. It's just a pull-start Johnson 15, a simple two-stroke engine. Long as it's got a fuel supply and a clean spark plug it ought to run like a top. It hasn't been used in a while so the carburetor might be dirty, but that's not an issue—especially for a top carburetor mechanic like you," Mitch grinned.

"Well, if it *does* run, are you saying we can get it to the river with that old tractor?"

"Of course. Like I said, it'll pull a trailer just fine. It won't run but about 15 miles per hour down the road, but that beats walking, and we can put all our stuff in the boat and haul everything we need."

"I wish we could just drive it to Hattiesburg," April sighed. "But all the other refugees will see us coming. And I'm sure there will be more roadblocks like the one we already went through. Things are bound to be getting worse by the day."

Mitch nodded. "We need to slip in by the back door, and that back door is the river. Like you saw from the map, it's only about fifteen miles from here to the closest point on the Leaf from which we can launch. Once we get this tractor running and get hitched up, we can be there in about an hour and a half if we don't run into trouble. Then, we launch the boat and head upriver. It's about thirty-five to forty river miles with all the bends between where we'll launch and Hattiesburg. This little outboard isn't fast, but even so, it shouldn't take more than three or four hours. We'll time it so we're running at night—less chance of running into anybody on the river that way."

"I hope you mean *tonight*," April said.

"Of course. It's only about one in the afternoon right now. There's a lot to do, but we've got time if we get busy."

SIXTEEN

Mitch and April worked through most of the afternoon making preparations to travel once again. This trip would be a lot different. They would be much more prepared with food supplies, detailed maps, camping gear, and—most comforting of all—good weapons to defend themselves with. But before they began gathering their supplies, the first thing Mitch did was bag up all the rotting meat from the freezers in heavy-duty trash bags and haul them out to a ditch in the woods opposite the cow pasture. The coyotes and vultures would make short work of that, and he figured the smell in the house would eventually dissipate. Then he lit some scented candles from his mom's bathroom to make it more tolerable inside as they sorted through the remaining nonperishable foods and other stuff they would need.

Getting the tractor going took longer than they expected. It had not been used for a while, so the battery was dead and the tires were nearly flàt. Mitch was able to start it by jumping it off with the fresh, heavy-duty battery he removed from his dad's state truck, and he and April took turns with a bicycle pump to bring the big rear tires of the tractor and boat trailer up to an acceptable pressure.

There was enough diesel in two jerry cans stored in the barn to nearly fill the tractor's fuel tank, and once again using his Mississippi Credit Card trick—this time cutting a piece of old hose from his mom's garden—he siphoned enough regular gasoline from the Trailblazer and the truck to run the small outboard. Between the large portable gas tank in his dad's patrol boat and several smaller gas cans used for the lawnmower, he was able to round up a supply that he was sure would be more than enough to run the little John boat up the Leaf River to Hattiesburg and back. The old Johnson was the two-stroke type, requiring a mixture of oil with the gasoline, but that was no issue as there was plenty of two-stroke oil around the Henley farm for use in the weed-eaters, chainsaws, and other tools.

"Ever drove a tractor?" Mitch asked April, after he backed it into position and hitched the boat trailer to it.

"You ought to know the answer to that, but I'll bet I can figure it out."

"Yeah, I guess you haven't had many opportunities to cut hay where you grew up. Here, give it a try." Mitch showed her the throttle, clutch, and shifter and stepped down after she settled into the seat. "Just take it easy and pull around right in front of the house. We'll load everything in the boat and get going."

Mitch watched as she pulled off smoothly with the boat in tow. He knew she was in a hurry to get to her daughter, but every minute she was still hanging out with him was a good one, as far as he was concerned. He dreaded their inevitable parting, which would come soon enough despite the setbacks that had kept her with him this long. Even though the journey to Hattiesburg would give him more time with her, it wouldn't be much, and then he would have to face the fact that he had no idea how he was going to find Lisa, Stacy, and Jason.

They could be anywhere. They might be in Hattiesburg looking for Stacy and Jason's mom if they had not already found her, back at the Burns' house in Brooklyn, or anywhere in between. Mitch knew that traveling there in these conditions to look for three or four people was like looking for a needle in a haystack. Never mind the difficulty of actually getting somewhere without cars and trucks, it was the loss of instant communication that made everything seem so impossible. If only he could call Lisa and find out where she was. Cell phones, even landlines, were a technology he had taken for granted just like everyone else.

As much as he fantasized about living back in frontier times when he could have been a full-time hunter and explorer, he realized how hard it must have been to go weeks, months, or even years without hearing from loved ones left behind. He and April would completely miss Lisa and her friends if they were traveling back to the farm by road while the two of them were in the boat going upriver. He didn't know what to do, but it didn't seem to make any more sense to him to sit here and wait, either. They might not ever come back, or if they did, it might take days or even longer.

He would leave a note outlining his travel plan in case they did return in the meantime, but beyond that, the only thing that seemed logical now was to help April get back to her child. She had tried to help him, and he had promised her a ride if she came this far with him. Now he intended to deliver whether he had the old Ford truck or not.

After what they'd already seen, he felt better about traveling on the river than the road anyway. They might encounter a few people using the waterway, as there were a lot of old, simple outboards still in use around these parts. And, unlike Black Creek, more camps and full-time homes were scattered along the Leaf. Still, he felt like they would have a good chance of getting through to Hattiesburg if they traveled by night. There would still be plenty of moonlight, as the moon was just two days past full, and the Leaf was big enough to navigate safely at night at the kind of speeds the little Johnson 15 would be capable of.

With the boat in front of the house, they went back inside to get groceries, the camping gear, cookware, and a supply of ammo for all the weapons. There was no way they could take all the firearms, especially the specialized hunting weapons he and his dad owned, and he wouldn't have wanted to anyway. Between the .22 rifle and his bow, getting food wouldn't be a problem, though he didn't expect to have to hunt until he got back anyway considering how much food they were taking with them from his mom's pantry.

It would be good to have a stash of weapons and ammo here for later if something happened to the ones he picked to take, and he felt pretty good about the gun safe—for now anyway. If the house was left unattended long enough, someone would eventually clean it out, but he didn't intend for that to happen. Before he locked it back up, he asked April to look through the handguns. When she picked up a compact Sig Sauer 9mm that she said felt good in her hands, he told her that it was hers to keep, along with the Ruger carbine.

"I can't do that," April said. "I know how expensive these are. I don't know how I would pay for them, unless David has some cash on him when we get there."

"Cash isn't good for much by now anyway, I don't reckon. Don't worry about that. If the lights ever come back on and things get back to normal, maybe we can settle up then. Right now there's no one else I'd rather give these to than you, and no one I know who needs them more. I've got that bow for you, too, back here in my room."

He led her into his bedroom where he knew she would be shocked to see that almost all the wall space was taken up by racks of various bows and arrows, some store-bought and many homemade attempts at copying various Native American and other types of bows used by primitive cultures he'd studied.

"Wow! Now I can see why you're so good with that thing. You're obsessed!"

"Yeah, I guess you could say that."

"I don't mean it in a bad way. I think it's really cool."

Mitch picked a simple longbow that he'd used when he was younger, an inexpensive but good shooting fiberglass-composite with a draw weight of forty-pounds at twenty-eight inches. He strung it and let April try it. It was clear that she could handle it much better than his sixty-pound hunting bow. He picked a shoulder quiver and selected a dozen cedar shafts tipped with broadheads and fletched with turkey feathers. They were perfectly matched to the bow and with a little practice he was sure she would get good with it quickly.

April was again apologetic in accepting such an offer, but Mitch dismissed her objections and countered with his own apology, wishing they would have more time for him to teach her what he knew. He didn't completely dismiss the hope that there *would* be a way he could spend more time with her, but he didn't want to let her know he was thinking that or dwell on it too much himself.

They then went through the pantry and sorted through the canned goods, bags of rice, packages of pasta, and hot cereals. He noticed that Lisa had naturally cleaned out all the ready-to-eat stuff like the boxes of cold cereals, bags of chips, and other snacks. He could only hope she and her friends had taken some real food, too. They put all this stuff in a large canvas duffle bag, and Mitch carried it out to the boat. He put the extra ammo for the various weapons they were taking in a large waterproof box, and another duffle bag held a skillet, cooking pot, utensils, a small propane stove, and two sleeping bags packed in their stuff sacks. Once they tied everything down so it would ride without falling out of the boat along the road, they were ready. Mitch locked the house, leaving his note for Lisa on the dining table inside. The sun was already low by this time, its rays filtering through the perimeter pines that cast long shadows across the lawn.

"If we go now, we'll just make it to the river before dark. Why don't you drive the tractor, and I'll stand on the deck beside you and ride shotgun," he said, holding up the Remington 870.

"Yeah, like *literally*," she laughed. "Fine by me, long as you tell me where to go."

Mitch looked back over his shoulder as April steered the old International tractor down the lane leading out to the road. He hoped it wouldn't be long before he could return, but the way things were going there was no telling. He thought about his mom and dad and wondered again if it were possible that their plane had crashed before they landed in Houston. It was something he had been trying not to think about. Instead, he focused on the image of them making their way back here somehow—a journey that would be extremely difficult and dangerous but nevertheless much better than that other possibility.

When they reached the end of the gravel lane, he directed April to turn right on the narrow county road that ran roughly parallel to Black Creek. They would stay on this one until they came to another county road that would take them to the only bridge that crossed the creek for many miles in either direction. The road that passed by the Henley farm was completely deserted, as it usually was even in normal times, as there were no other houses nearby and the piney woods started just beyond the edge of the right-of-way on either side. There were no abandoned cars here, and Mitch hadn't expected to see any. But as they rounded the first bend, a short distance past the property line, he saw what he had feared he would eventually be seeing a lot of: someone on foot in the middle of the road. It was a male figure, but that's all he could tell from the distance. Whoever it was, he was apparently injured, *Or at least pretending to be*, Mitch thought. The man was hobbling along unsteadily with what looked like a tree branch used as a makeshift crutch.

"What should I do?" April asked as she glanced at Mitch.

"Slow it way down," he said, even though they were already going barely over 10 mph. "He could be armed. Keep it slow but don't stop until we get close enough to get a better look."

"He looks hurt, but it might be a trap," she said, echoing Mitch's thoughts. She eased off the throttle and brought the tractor to a crawl.

"You're right. Wait until I tell you, then stop and stay here where you can cover me with the rifle while I hop off and see who it is and what he's up to. I don't like it that he's heading in the direction of the house."

Mitch racked the slide on the shotgun to chamber a round before they got closer. The figure in the road had stopped, and lifted an arm with what appeared to be a great effort, attempting a friendly wave. Then he collapsed to his knees, apparently so weak it was all he could do to stand, much less walk. Mitch told April to stop when they were about 50 yards away, and when she took the tractor out of gear she picked up her rifle as Mitch stepped down to the ground.

He moved forward cautiously, holding the shotgun at hip level and ready until he was close enough to see that the man in the road wasn't carrying a weapon or anything else. He wasn't even wearing any shoes, just a pair of blue jeans and a flannel shirt that was blood-ied and torn. It was clear that this wasn't a ruse—who-ever this guy was he was really hurt. Mitch lowered the shotgun and quickly covered the rest of the distance to the injured man.

He had longish, sandy blond hair that was vaguely familiar, and when Mitch squatted by his side to ask him what happened, he saw that he had been mistaken in thinking this was a stranger, some wandering refugee that had somehow found his way to this remote country road. Beneath the two black eyes and cut and bleeding lips, was the face not of an older man, as he was sure he would see, but of a boy his own age.

"Jason!" Mitch exclaimed in shock. "Jason! What happened? Where are Lisa and Stacy?"

SEVENTEEN

April leapt down from the tractor, leaving the engine running at idle and grabbed one of the bottles of water they had stashed in the John boat. She had not heard what he said to the person in the road, but it was clear that Mitch wanted to help him and that he needed water. With the rifle slung over her shoulder, she hurried to his side.

"What happened to him, do you know him?"

"April, this is Jason! Lisa's best friend's brother, the one they were with. I don't know what happened yet. He's so dehydrated he's just barely mumbling. Give me the water!"

April couldn't believe what she was hearing. She opened the water bottle and handed it to Mitch, squatting down beside him and looking at the battered face that she could now see was younger than she'd expected. Whoever did this had nearly beaten him to death. In addition to the blows to his face, his right hand was swollen and blue, with broken bones likely, and his left leg was twisted and looked like it had been broken or his knee dislocated. He was begging for water when Mitch held the bottle to his lips and wiped away some of the blood from his face with his other hand.

"Jason, you've got to tell me what happened. Where is my sister? Where is your sister? Who did this to you? What did they do to them?"

"Took them," Jason sputtered. "I tried to stop them. I tried to fight them."

"Who took them?" Mitch asked, his voice trembling with panic. "Who were they, Jason? Where's the truck? Were you all in it?"

"Took the truck, too. I couldn't do anything. They were just waiting for somebody to come along. They had it planned out."

"Who did?" Mitch asked. "Where did this happen? How long ago?"

Mitch gave him another drink of water and waited for him to swallow so he could answer. April could see the rage and fear in Mitch's eyes, and looking at the condition Jason was in, she totally understood. Anyone capable of hurting someone this badly was capable of anything.

"I don't know them," Jason said. "Never seen any of them before, but when they first came out of the woods, Lisa said three of them were brothers, Wallace brothers."

"Wallace! Wallace brothers? Are you serious?"

April looked at him with the obvious question.

"Scumbags!" Mitch said. "Bunch of outlaw redneck scumbags! My dad has arrested every one of them half a dozen times. Headlighting deer, poaching alligators, cooking meth, stolen vehicles and ATVs, you name it. When they're not in jail it's almost a full-time job for Dad to just keep track of them."

"They're brothers? How many of them are there?"

"I don't know, three or four. Their dad's just as bad as they are. There are always some uncles and cousins or nephews or something hanging around with them. You don't see one or even two without seeing at least a couple more. I don't know how many people live out at that place, but they're real lowlifes, all of them. They've got about forty acres of cutover bottom land over on a branch on the north side of Black Creek with a bunch of old trailers and shacks all over the place. Junk cars and all kinds of crap everywhere there's not a tree in the way." Mitch turned back to Jason. "Where did you run into them? How long ago was this?"

"It was the day before yesterday, late in the evening," Jason said. "I guess about this time of day. We had gotten to your house that morning after walking all the way from our house in Brooklyn. We went there to borrow that old truck, because Lisa said your dad wouldn't mind and we'd seen a couple of other antique cars running since the blackout. We were going to Hattiesburg to get my mom. She was working there when all this happened and couldn't get home."

"That's what we figured you had done," Mitch said.

"I'm sorry. If it hadn't been my idea to try to go get my mom, none of this would have happened."

"Just tell me what they did," Mitch said. "Did they hurt my little sister like they hurt you?"

April put a hand on Mitch's shoulder as he trembled with dread while questioning Jason. She could only imagine what he was going through.

"We were on the other side of the creek, not far across the bridge. I was driving and when I went around a bend, all of a sudden there was a huge pine tree lying across the road. I could tell somebody had cut it down deliberately. I stopped and was going to turn around when these three men just stepped out of the woods on either side of the road behind us, with their deer rifles pointed right at us. Lisa had your dad's patrol rifle, but it wouldn't have done any good to try anything. They already had the drop on us. It happened so fast and was so unexpected; there was just nothing we could do.

"They told us to get out of the truck. I knew as soon as I saw them with their guns that it was the truck they wanted. They had blocked the road and were just waiting and hoping someone would come along with a running vehicle. I guess we were pretty close to where they lived, because they must have walked there. I thought they would just take the truck and leave us alone. But then two more of them came out from the other side of the roadblock—two older-looking men with long, wild beards and scraggly hair. They looked like brothers, too, just like the three younger ones did.

"They started asking us all kinds of questions and Lisa got really mad. She said her dad was the game warden and if they took that truck they would never hunt in his county again when he got through with them. That's when it really got ugly. I guess Lisa should have kept her mouth shut. When they found out who she was, everything changed.

"One of the two older ones, the two really rough-looking ones, walked up to the truck like he was going to get in it and then he just all of a sudden punched me in the face. I never saw it coming. I remember hearing Lisa or Stacy scream, and then one of the younger ones, one of the three who had first stepped out of the woods, came over and kicked me in the head before I could get up from the first punch. I kept trying to get up, and both of them kept kicking me. Then I tried to crawl under the truck on my hands and knees, and one of them stomped on my hand with a heavy boot. I think it's broken. When I rolled over he stomped on my knee. He must've crushed my kneecap or something. I can't put any weight on it."

April shuddered. She couldn't imagine the pain he must have felt as it was happening, and the pain he must still be feeling now. It was going to take some time for him to recover, both from the physical damage and the emotional anguish of knowing he had utterly failed to defend the two younger girls. Mitch was in agony, too, agony along with shock and he felt fear as he listened to Jason's account of the attack.

"Did they hit Lisa and Stacy like that?"

"I don't know. I know they grabbed them. I could hear them screaming and the men yelling at them to shut up. I was almost to the point of passing out, but I remember hearing the truck drive off. They turned it around and went back the way we came and then turned off somewhere. I could hear the engine for a while, then I think I passed out.

"I don't know how long I was lying there. When I woke up, I couldn't believe I was still alive. It was barely breaking daylight. There was nothing in sight but the road and the woods and nothing to be heard but a few squirrels and birds. I crawled to the side of the road and eventually managed to sit up. I was thirsty and could taste nothing in my mouth but blood.

"I finally found this stick in the edge of the woods and managed to get up with it. I started back in the direction of your house, because that's all I knew to do. I needed water really bad, but all I found was a filthy puddle on the side of the road. I was able to wash my face some in it, and I drank just a little, but the water was nasty."

"So that was yesterday, when you woke up, and you've been trying to get back here since then? Two days?"

"In his condition he couldn't have gone far in two days," April said. "I'm surprised he was able to move at all."

"If this happened where I think it did, not far from the Wallace place, then that's about six or seven miles from here," Mitch said. "But I'm not worried about that. I'm worried about what they've done to Lisa and Stacy. Tonight will be the third night since this happened. I've got to go get them."

"How?" April asked. "It sounds like there are several of them, and they are all armed. There may be more that weren't at the roadblock, too."

"I don't care if there are a hundred. I'm getting my sister. And Jason's sister."

"I'm going, too," Jason said. "All I need is a gun. That's why I was going back to your place. I knew there was a gun safe there, and I was going to break into it one way or another and go back to kill those bastards."

"You're in no condition to do anything," April said. "You've got a lot of healing to do. You can barely walk, much less fight. I'll go with Mitch. Two of us will have a better chance than one."

April saw the look of surprise in Mitch's face. She knew he wouldn't ask her to do something like that, especially since she had already been delayed getting back to Kimberly so many times.

"April, I can't let you do that," Mitch said. "It's far too dangerous and . . ."

But April cut him off. "I can't let you go alone to face all those men. Do you think I could just go on to Hattiesburg with those two teenaged girls in the hands of those cretins? There is no question about it. I'm going."

April wasn't giving him further opportunity to argue with her. She would go with him and they would give the men who inflicted this much pain on others a taste of their own medicine, just as they had done to the three who had attacked her on the highway. But first, they needed to figure out what to do about Jason. He needed medical attention, but that was impossible.

"We take him back to the house," Mitch said. "That's all we can do. There's food and water and he'll be relatively safe there until we get back. We can't go driving up there with this tractor towing a boat anyway, so we might as well take it back there. Besides, we'll need that canoe we left down at the creek."

"Canoe?"

"Yes. The Wallace place is on a small tributary that runs into Black Creek from the north side. We can reach it by paddling downstream about five miles from where we left the canoe. We can paddle up the branch a little ways, then we'll have to leave the boat and go on foot. One thing about doing it this way is that we'll be approaching their place from behind, where there's nothing but woods and swamp. They'll never expect that, and besides, I doubt they're expecting anyone to come for the girls anyway. They left Jason there to die and probably figure he did. They'll be watching the road out front, of course, but not that little branch down in the woods, especially not at night."

"At night? Do you mean tonight?" April asked.

"Hell yes, tonight! As soon as we can get there! You don't know how hard it is for me to resist the temptation to just drive this tractor straight there right now with this shotgun blasting. But I know I've got to be smart about this. I can't take any chances that Lisa or Stacy might be hit by a stray bullet in a gunfight, or that they won't simply use them as hostages once they figure out what's happening. No, it's got to be a total surprise, an attack coming out of nowhere. Hit them hard before they know they're being hit, and the best way to do that is to go tonight. But it will be easier to sneak in there in the dark, and we've got all night to do it. We just need to get Jason up in that boat and pull the trailer back to the house."

"I want to go," Jason said. "This is all my fault."

"It's not your fault," Mitch said. "It's those sons of bitches' faults. They are opportunists, just like a lot of others that are taking advantage of this situation. They deserve what they're going to get, just like the three that made the mistake of messing with April here. Sorry I didn't introduce you, but we'll fill in the details later."

"Good to meet you, April," Jason said. "I'm sure you're plenty tough, but I've got to go with y'all. You need my help, too."

"Out of the question," Mitch said. "You can't even walk. We'll have to go a half-mile or more on foot, in the dark and without making a sound. Besides, there's only room for two of us in the canoe. We're going to get you to the house and get you something to eat and a weapon so you can defend yourself if anyone shows up, then April and I are going to be on our way, if she really wants to get into this," he said as he looked at her again.

"Nothing could stop me," April said.

"Then let's get going. You get one arm and I'll get the other. Let's get Jason loaded up and get out of here."

EIGHTEEN

April climbed up into the John boat on the trailer with Jason while Mitch drove the tractor, running it wide-open back the way they'd come as fast as it would go until he turned back into the lane and pulled up in front of the house again. It was almost dark by then, and together he and April helped Jason inside as quickly as possible. There was little time to do much for him other than try and make him somewhat comfortable and fix him something hot to eat. They guided him to Mitch's bedroom, then Mitch gathered all the candles he could find in the house and placed them within reach on the nightstand. He opened the gun safe again and got out his old Savage 20-gauge pump and a couple of boxes of shells for it so that Jason would not be unarmed while he waited for them to get back. April unpacked the propane stove Mitch had stashed in the boat, and using a big pot from the kitchen, heated several cans of vegetable soup all mixed together so they could all share a meal before the two of them left on their rescue mission.

Mitch and April both agreed upon closer examination that none of Jason's injuries were life-threatening, but the broken bones in his hand and his shattered knee would take lots of time to heal, and they'd probably never be right again without proper medical care. Mitch didn't know what to do about that, but there was no time to be concerned with it. He was lucky to be alive at all, and Mitch was honestly quite surprised that those Wallace brothers didn't simply shoot him before they left with the girls and the truck. At least he and April had gotten him off the road and brought him someplace safe. With food and water available, he would be okay until they returned.

When they had finished eating, Mitch went back outside to sort out what they would need for their nighttime raid on the Wallace place. He was taking the Remington 870, of course, and he filled his pockets with extra double-aught buckshot shells and a few slugs. Just like his dad, he felt better about using the shotgun in the dark than any rifle, and he expected that when he did use it tonight, it would be at close range. He thought about getting another shotgun for April, but since she was more familiar with the rifle's light recoil, she would be better off with it. He hoped he wouldn't even need her help, but it was nice to know she had a weapon she was familiar with and would have his back if something went wrong.

The .357 Magnum was still on his belt, of course, and he slung his quiver of broadhead-tipped arrows over his shoulder opposite the shotgun sling and picked up his hunting bow—the same one he'd been carrying. He was not about to attempt anything this dangerous without it. Silence was a big factor in maintaining the element of surprise that might enable the two of them to pull this off, despite being outnumbered.

He went back inside and checked to see that April had her spare magazine for the Mini 14, and then he sorted out a few other essentials, like his hunting knife, compass, two small battery-powered flashlights, water-proof matches, and a canteen in which they could carry a small supply of drinking water to get them through the night. April was still wearing the clothes she'd had on when they met. She could move okay in them, but the shirt was too bright for a nighttime raid like this. Mitch went to his mom's room to find something else.

"You'd better change into this," he said. "I think it will fit you okay." He handed her a plain black sweatshirt that his mom liked to wear when she went for walks.

"We'll have to sneak up pretty close, won't we?"

"Yes. You, not so much, with that rifle, but I want to be in bow range before they even know we're there. You can cover me, but I think I can hit them before they know what's happening."

"I suppose we won't be asking them to give us back the truck and release Lisa and Stacy, then?"

"No," Mitch said. "I don't plan on asking them anything. After you go in there and change, I've got something else that will help, too." He held it up for her to see.

"What is that?"

"Camouflage makeup. We'll use it to black out our faces. Faces shine at night like you wouldn't believe. They're a dead giveaway. They use it in the military, especially in the Special Forces. Some bow-hunters use it, too, especially hunting turkeys, because they have such good eyesight. That's what I have it for. The deer hunters around here mostly shoot from long range in an elevated shooting house, so they don't bother."

"I'm all for it then if it'll help us sneak in. I sure don't want to get shot at."

"Me neither. Not if there's anyway I can help it. Here, I'll put it on your face if you'll do mine. That'd be easier than trying to do it in the mirror with candlelight."

Mitch waited while April went in the other room and changed her shirt. When she came back, she walked up and stood close to him, pulling her hair back away from her face with both hands and looking him directly in the eye, causing him to feel that old familiar unease he always felt when in close proximity to a girl—especially one as attractive as April.

"How much experience do you have doing a girl's makeup?" she asked.

"Exactly none," Mitch said. "Well, I put this stuff on my sister once when we were playing hide and seek."

"I trust you can get it right. Go ahead, paint me up."

Mitch squeezed some of the dark green cream from one of the tubes onto his index finger and reached out to gently apply two broad strips on each of her cheekbones. He fought to keep his hand from trembling as he felt the smooth silkiness of her skin under his fingertip. "It's paint all right," he said. "War paint." He overcame his nervousness at the thought of how serious what they were about to undertake really was, and how much was at stake. He followed the green with a few more dabs and streaks of black, so that when he was done, April's face was mottled and dark, with nothing bright remaining except her blue-green eyes.

"Okay, my turn to paint," she said. Mitch stood as still as he could while she made her careful and delicate strokes. He was sure she was doing a better job than he did, but that's not what he was thinking about. Her touch took away any thoughts he might have had about camouflage paint. Once again he found himself strug-gling to hide the effect she had on him. It was so incred-ibly unfair to finally have met such a beautiful girl who was so outgoing, tough, and resourceful, and that he could find so much in common with, only to know that he would never have a chance with her because she was already taken—the mother of another man's child.

When she was done, she took him by the hand and pulled him to the bathroom mirror. "Oh my God," she said, when she saw her own face in the candlelight. "I look like the creature from the Black Lagoon, crossed with Rambo!"

Mitch looked at his own green and black mask, curv-ing, symmetrical lines and concentric circles like the facial tattoos of a Maori warrior. It was much more so-phisticated than the streaks and blobs he had painted on April. If one of those Wallace brothers saw that face in the firelight, he would likely have a heart attack, but Mitch was counting on none of them seeing a thing.

"Okay, it's time to go," he said. They went back to where Jason was resting on Mitch's bed. "We're on our way out," Mitch said. "I'll be back as soon as possible, but not without Lisa and Stacy, no matter how long it takes."

They left the house with Mitch leading the way into the field beyond the barn, going back to Black Creek the same way they'd come when he'd brought her here after they stashed the canoe. Mitch could hardly believe that all had happened earlier that very day. Time was really getting distorted in this new reality, as each day was packed full of so many events and decisions that the days seemed as long as weeks had in the old world of mundane, everyday life.

There was enough starlight and he knew the way well enough that they did not have to turn on the small L.E.D. flashlights they carried until they reached the edge of the woods. He had warned April that they were absolutely not to use them once they reached the creek. Out on the water, he knew he could see well enough to navigate by starlight, and the moon would be up later when they made their way up the tributary that ran by the Wallace place.

Mitch could have found his way to the place they left the canoe even without the flashlights if he had to. He had no fear of the dark and often wandered the woods of their land at night, especially in cooler weather when there was no worry of stepping on a nocturnal rattle-snake. The danger of snakes was the only reason that he even brought the lights, but he didn't want to worry April with that, so he just told her to stick close and walk right behind him.

When they reached the big hardwood trees of the bottomlands close to the creek, a sudden sound like rushing wind, followed by the crashing of something heavy running through the pitch black forest caused April to grab Mitch by the arm and pull him to a stop near her.

Mitch suppressed a quiver at her sudden touch. "Just a deer blowing," he said. "They snort like that when they catch the scent of danger."

"Damn! I didn't know what that was. I thought it was a bear!" she whispered.

"I know. It is surprising the first time you hear it. There are all kinds of weird sounds out here at night, but once you know what they are, they're no big deal. The canoe should be right over here."

He took a silent, deep breath and led the way into a thicket of bay shrubs. The canoe was just as they'd left it, still covered with the branches and debris they'd piled on to make it less obvious. They flipped it over so they could grab the carry handles at each end. Mitch took the bow and guided them through the underbrush and down the slope the rest of the way to the banks of the creek. When they emerged from the forest, the gurgling waters of the creek shimmered and sparkled in the faint starlight. Mitch slid the canoe in and held it steady while April climbed to the bow, inadvertently allowing the butt stock of the Ruger carbine to bang loudly against the aluminum gunwale.

"Sorry!" she whispered. "I'll be more careful next time."

"It's okay," he whispered back. "It's not likely there's anyone anywhere near here. But when we get down to that branch, we're going to have to be super quiet. It'd be best to take that rifle off your shoulder and lay it down carefully in the bottom. That way that won't happen again."

"Okay."

Mitch placed his own weapons in the hull in front of him and slipped into the stern seat, using his paddle to push off from the sandy shallows. When the canoe floated free, he steered it out to midstream where there was the most light, and then began a slow but steady stroke to get them moving downriver. It was too dark to go at maximum speed, even though that was relatively slow in a canoe like this. There were too many snags and other obstructions in the current that could capsize an unwary paddler, and though he was anxious to get to Lisa as soon as possible, he knew better than to take foolish chances and mess up everything by dumping the boat and losing their weapons. Besides, even at a careful pace, they would get to the tributary in less than two hours. Mitch wasn't sure exactly how far they would have to walk from there to reach the Wallace place, but the road they lived on wasn't much more than a mile from Black Creek, so he knew it couldn't be too far.

Because of the darkness, he asked April not to paddle, but instead to help him look for obstructions from her vantage point in the bow. Listening to the sound of the running water was as useful to him in the dark as trying to see, and he didn't want the dipping of her paddle drowning out the sounds of subtle changes in the current that could tell him where shoals or underwater logs were. They rounded bend after bend in silence until the stillness was shattered by a huge splash that sounded like a cannonball plunging into the water ahead. The splash startled April, and Mitch could see her suddenly stiffen in the seat in front of him. He didn't blame her. The forest and river was an alien environment to her, especially in the dark.

"Was that an alligator or something? It had to be something huge!" she whispered.

"Just a beaver," he whispered back. "They slap the water like that with their tails. It's amazing that an animal that small can make such a splash, but they do."

Another half hour or so after the beaver splash, Mitch figured they were getting close to the mouth of the little tributary. He kept a close watch on the left bank as he paddled, knowing it was small and didn't look like much from the creek. He'd never explored this one as he had many such branches that fed the creek, mainly because it ran through the Wallace place and other private lands rather than national forestlands not far upstream. His dad had also warned him to avoid it specifically because of those people, saying they weren't likely to change no matter how many times he carried them to jail. When Mitch finally spotted the opening in the bank to his left, he steered the canoe beneath the trees that hung low overhead and let the bow slide up into the soft mix of mud and sand where the waters merged.

"This is it," he whispered, in an even lower tone than he'd used while they were floating downstream. Mitch stepped out into the ankle-deep water and walked up onto the bank. The moon was just now filtering through the trees at a low angle, and in its light he could see that the small bar of white sand was unmarked by human footprints.

"It doesn't look like anyone's been down here recently. Let's wait right here for another hour or so until the moon gets higher. It's going to be a lot darker up this branch than out on the main creek. We need enough light to see so we don't go breaking sticks and stuff busting through the woods."

While they waited, they sat on the sandbar and discussed what they were about to do in low whispers. If he had not already seen how coolly April handled herself in the face of danger, he would not have wanted to put her in this situation. But he knew he could count on her, and other than his dad, he didn't know anyone else who could do a better job of it than she could.

"We've got to move really slowly when we go up this creek to make sure we are utterly silent in our approach. I'm not sure how far it is, but at a stalking pace like that, it could take an hour to go a quarter of a mile. We'll really have to slow down once we know we are in the vicinity of their place."

"Do you think they'll be inside asleep? How will we get to Lisa and Stacy if they are?"

"I don't know yet. We're just going to have to get there first and watch the houses and trailers without being seen, see if they are doing anything. If they are inside, it will be more difficult. We may have to create a diversion to draw them out. All we can do is get up there and see what's going on."

When the amount of moonlight reaching the forest floor was sufficient to allow them to move quietly, they decided that it would be best to go all the way on foot, rather than try to paddle part way up the branch. He pulled the canoe a few yards upstream so that it wouldn't be visible from Black Creek and tied it off to a tree.

April checked to make sure she had a round chambered in her rifle, and Mitch slung the bow over his shoulder. They nodded in silent agreement to move out. Mitch led the way forward, keeping the shotgun at the ready in case of any surprises along the way. He asked April to stick close behind him and to try to step where he stepped since she was unskilled in stalking and would not know how to pick her steps through the undergrowth, especially at night. By keeping her close behind him, he could also gently release the springy branches that he frequently had to bend out of the way so they could pass, without risking her getting slapped in the face by one.

They moved like this for maybe ten steps at a time, before stopping to listen, sometimes pausing several minutes before moving again. He knew this would seem excruciatingly slow to April, who had lived at the pace of the city all her life, but this time a careful approach was more critical than it had ever been on any hunting trip. It was a matter of life or death.

Before leaving the canoe, they had already agreed on complete voice silence. Not even a whisper was permitted except in the direst emergency. Keeping her that close behind him, Mitch could reach back to stop her with his free hand if they suddenly needed to freeze for some reason.

By the time they had repeated this move-and-stop cycle maybe two dozen times, more than an hour had passed. Mitch stopped longer than usual and motioned for April to do the same. While they waited this time, they heard something else besides the usual night sounds of crickets and tree frogs. It was the sound of laughter off in the distance, a man's laughter, followed by a shout in a different male voice. Mitch felt the hairs on the back of his neck rise. He tightened his grip on the shotgun, feeling the adrenaline rush brought on by certainty of an imminent fight.

NINETEEN

The sound of the distant laughter and shouting from out of the dark forest caused April to tense. Until now, this nighttime trek by canoe and on foot had only been a bit spooky. Now the reality of what they were about to do hit her in the face as she heard the echoing voices of what could only be the men from the Wallace place— the men who had brutally beaten Jason and taken Lisa and Stacy. She gripped the rifle tighter in her hands and hoped she would not fail under pressure—that she could continue to live up to the confidence Mitch had in her and not let him down when it really counted.

Though she had been surprised at how well she had defended herself against the three men on the road and when facing that angry landowner's rifle, this would be the first time she had ever participated in an out-right attack on someone else. Mitch had stressed that in order to rescue the girls in this situation, they would have to strike ruthlessly and without remorse. They were outnumbered from the beginning and could not afford to let men such as these surrender. It would be far too risky to try to simply point guns at these men and demand they release the girls. April knew he was right, and knew all the rules had changed since the blackout. This was essentially war, and they had to do whatever was required in order to win. She just hoped she wouldn't lose her nerve when it came time to pull the trigger.

When they started moving again, Mitch led the way, pausing every third or fourth step to listen. April found that by walking carefully and deliberately, she, too, could move with surprising silence. The nearby running water helped, too, as its gurgling sound would drown out the noise of a minor misstep. The voices were intermittent, but every few minutes they heard them get louder and laugh. To April, it sounded like the men were likely drinking and carrying on. She figured it must be getting close to midnight, but without TV or other entertainment, they probably had little else to do out here.

The voices became clearer as they painstakingly made their way closer, following the little stream. They were all men, from what she could tell. She didn't know if it was a good sign or a bad one that she didn't hear any voices that could be Lisa's or Stacy's. Was it possible that they had already killed them? Maybe they never even brought them back to where they lived and had disposed of the bodies somewhere along the way?

She quickly dismissed the thought. If that were the case, they probably would have done what they were going to do right at the scene of the roadblock and done the same to Jason. It surprised her that they left him alive. She assumed it was because they were confident he would not be able to make it anywhere for help, or else they were just incredibly stupid. Or maybe there were enough of them that they simply weren't worried who found out what they were doing. She sincerely hoped this was not the case.

The under story of the forest along the little stream was dense with bay thickets and other vegetation, requiring them to bend and weave their way through very slowly to avoid making noise. Because of this density, it was not until they were quite close that they could see the flickering flames of a fire. Mitch continued creeping closer and April followed. As they closed the distance they could see that the fire was situated between them and some buildings, the flames casting their light on what looked like a wooden cabin and, next to it, a narrow mobile home with white aluminum siding. Parked between the cabin and the trailer was an antique-looking truck. She couldn't tell if it was a Ford or not, but she figured it was, and that it was proof these were the men who had taken it from Jason.

Just inside the edge of the woods, she could also see an old camper trailer that looked like it hadn't been on the road in years. But April wasn't focused on any of these objects, not even the truck. From this distance she could clearly see the men who were laughing and talking, some of them standing and walking around the circle of firelight and others sitting on stumps or old chairs pulled up nearby. She did a quick count as she looked on—four standing and three sitting, unless there were others she couldn't see in the shadows farther away from the fire. One of the men sitting on a stump had a rifle or shotgun across his lap. She saw a couple more long guns leaning against nearby trees. Most of them were drinking from what looked like beer cans but there was a liquor bottle being passed around, too. She didn't see any evidence of the two girls or any other females in the camp. Mitch turned and crouched very close beside her to whisper:

"Looks like at least seven of them. But I'm not ruling out the possibility there are more inside. If Lisa and Stacy are there, they'll be in that cabin or the trailer home."

"Is that your grandpa's truck?"

"Yes. That's the truck and those are clearly the men who took it."

"So, how are we going to do this?"

"Here's what I'm thinking: They're drinking a lot of beer and whiskey, it looks like. I've already seen one of them walk off into the woods behind that old camper; you probably noticed that, too. If I can get in position to use my bow to take out the next one who steps away from the fire to relieve himself, that'll be one less to worry about when the shooting starts. The main thing I want you to do is make sure your rounds don't go into that cabin or trailer. We can't risk hitting Lisa or Stacy. It would be better if you circle around to one side so that when you have to shoot, you'll have a clear line of fire without the buildings in the background. I'm going to sneak in closer straight ahead. I think I can get within thirty yards of them and still be in the cover of the woods but have a clear shot with the bow."

From where they were now, near the small stream, the land rose slightly to where the buildings and the fire were. It appeared that the side to the right of the buildings was a bit higher still, and the clearing around the trailer only extended some thirty or forty yards before ending in the edge of the woods. Mitch suggested April work her way around to that side, where she could shoot in the direction of the fire but parallel to the trailer and cabin to decrease the risk of hitting anyone inside.

"But what about you? How am I going to know you're out of the way?"

"You'll know," he whispered. "I don't want you to fire a shot until I start using the shotgun. When I do, I'll still be well away from the fire and in the woods. You'll probably see the flash from my muzzle blast. What I need you to do is concentrate on taking out any of them that try to take cover or get inside the buildings. I'll take care of anyone who heads for the woods. But like I said, I'm going to wait until one of them leaves the fire and use the bow first. I know I can take out one, maybe even two, before they know what's happening. You better go now, and get in position if you don't have any more questions. They may get tired and go inside any time."

"Okay, I'll do my best. Please be careful, Mitch." April reached out and put an arm around him, hugging him quickly. He did the same, pulling her close for a second and whispering a quick "thank you" in her ear for helping him.

"Remember, just two or three steps and stop, look, and listen, then move again. We're too close now to be in a hurry."

April nodded and started on her slow, meticulous stalk around to the uphill side of the camp. With each step she moved in slow motion, trying to feel the ground beneath her foot to make sure there was no branch or twig that would snap under her weight before putting it down. It seemed to take forever as she stepped and stopped, working her way around through the woods, staying deep in the shadows, but always close enough that she could see the fire and the men around it. They continued their conversation and laughter, oblivious of any danger. They probably thought they were immune to any retribution for what they'd done since everybody was focused on their own survival and law enforcement officers were few and far between. If they knew one of the girls was the daughter of the wildlife officer who had given them so much grief in the past, they must have gotten it out of her that he was not in area, otherwise they would be more cautious. But there was no way of knowing anything now. It was all just speculation until they searched the buildings and found out for sure whether or not the two girls were on the property.

April knew that Mitch wouldn't be able to see her beyond her first few steps. He had told her in advance he was going to estimate when twenty minutes had passed, and then he would assume she was in position, as he planned to be by that time as well. When she finally reached a point where she could see the men and fire with nothing behind them but woods, she decided she had gone far enough. The back walls of the cabin and the trailer were maybe twenty feet from the fire. She had a clear line of fire that would allow her to shoot any one of the men from where she was without any danger of hitting either building, unless of course by the bad luck of a ricochet. There was no way to completely eliminate that risk, though; all she could do was take careful aim and make each shot count.

She positioned herself beside the trunk of a thick pine tree and settled down on one knee to wait. She would use the tree to steady the rifle, as her dad had taught her—he'd always said it was better to use any kind of rest than none at all, if possible. She checked that she had a clear shot by bringing the rifle up to position and aiming it at each of the men in turn. The firelight lit them up and made each face stand out in the dark. Hitting any one of them would be a piece of cake, but April still wondered how hard it would be to actually pull the trigger when the time came.

As she watched, one of the men took a deep swig from his beer can, draining it dry before tossing it empty into the fire. He then said something she couldn't hear to the others and walked away from the circle, straight for the old abandoned camper at the edge of the dark woods right near where Mitch was supposed to be. April felt her stomach tense into knots and her hands begin to shake. It was about to begin.

* * *

She followed the movement of the man until he disappeared into the shadows. Just as Mitch had predicted, they were drinking a lot and it was inevitable they would all be making trips into the woods to relieve themselves. She wished she could see Mitch and the man whom would likely be the first to fall to his deadly arrows, but it was just too dark everywhere beyond the reach of the firelight and the man was on the other side of the camper now anyway. She waited and tried to control her breathing as she watched. If nothing happened, the man should be back in under a minute to get another beer and get back in on the joking and laughing with his buddies. But at least a minute went by, and he did not re-emerge from the dark woods. She waited and watched to see what the others would do. They were apparently oblivious at first, but minute after minute went by, and finally she heard a shout. It was from one of the men at the fire:

"Hey, Travis, what's taking you so long? You need some help finding it, or what?"

At this the rest of the men laughed. Another one yelled out something she couldn't quite make out, and they all laughed even harder. There was no response from the man behind the camper. Mitch must have been successful. She had not heard a thing—not the twang of a bowstring or the thwack of an arrow hitting flesh, and she knew that if she couldn't hear it from where she was, the others certainly couldn't over their loud carrying on and the crackling of the fire. She was watching with the rifle braced against the tree and ready, her gaze just above the iron sights and her finger resting on the flat steel of the trigger guard, ready and waiting.

"C'mon, Travis, what the hell are you doing?" It was the same man who had called out before. April couldn't tell much about his features from this distance, other than that he was tall and lanky, his face bearded and dark under the shadow of a baseball cap. When he got no response this time, he threw his own empty can down and picked up what looked like a shotgun leaning against the tree beside him. With the gun carried loosely in one hand, he walked away from the fire and disappeared from her view behind the camper just as the first one did. The others didn't bother to stop what they were doing, other than one who made a comment she heard clearly: "That's it, Charley. Go give him a hand!" This brought a roar of laughter that the second man behind the camper seemed to ignore.

April almost stopped breathing as she waited to see what was going to happen next. She moved her finger from outside the trigger guard to let it rest momentarily on the trigger, and then moved it back out again. As she did so, she moved her sights from one man to the next, wondering which one she would shoot first when the time came. She didn't have to wait long. Someone from the fire yelled again: "Charley! Travis!" The man who had been sitting on the stump with a gun across his lap got up and took a step toward the woods.

April saw him pause in midstride, then drop the gun and clutch at his chest. Even though she couldn't see it, she knew before he hit the ground that he had fallen to an arrow. If Mitch had already shot the first two, as she was sure he had, then that was three out of seven already down! The remaining four around the fire scarcely had a chance to see why the one had fallen before the night was shattered by the thundering roar of Mitch's 3-inch Magnum 12-gauge. The panic and confusion that ensued made it difficult for her to tell which of the men had been hit and which were still threats. She aimed as best she could and started pulling the trigger. All but one of the men were down in a matter of seconds, and he was trying to crawl under the trailer to take cover, having no idea which way the attack was coming from. April aimed again and squeezed the trigger. She saw him collapse but she fired two more rounds to make sure.

Her ears rang from the rifle reports when she stopped shooting and she heard little else. Mitch's shotgun was silent and not one of the men who'd been sitting or standing by the fire was still moving. April was about to step forward and call out to Mitch but a sudden scream froze her in her tracks. She raised her rifle again as a figure ran out to the fire from behind the trailers. She could see that it was a woman, and that she was dressed in nightclothes and unarmed. The woman fell to the ground beside the body of one of the men and wailed at the top of her lungs, oblivious of the danger of getting shot herself. April saw Mitch step from the woods into the circle of firelight, his shotgun at his hip and pointed at the woman. April stood and moved forward to join him, keeping her own weapon ready as she slowly made her way into the clearing.

TWENTY

When Mitch shot the first of the men who left the fire, he knew that if his aim was off and he didn't kill him instantly, the man might cry out in pain or even make his way back to the others to alert them. To decrease the chances of that happening, when he drew the bow he aimed squarely at the man's face, rather than his chest or neck, as he would have done if he were shooting a deer or other large animal with an arrow. He was confident in taking such a shot, because the distance to his target from where he was hiding was less than fifteen yards.

The man had stopped just out of sight of the others and unfastened his belt and opened his zipper. Mitch knew he would be standing still for several seconds, and while he was, he would be silhouetted perfectly against the background firelight. There was time to concentrate on the shot as Mitch held the bow at full draw. He felt no uneasiness or shaking this time, as he had that first time he'd killed a man with his bow. These men had taken his sister, and that was enough to give him a clear conscience, even without the knowledge of what they'd done to Jason and their history of run-ins with the law.

Unlike most modern bow-hunters who used modular broadhead hunting points with breakaway razorblade inserts, Mitch preferred a certain traditional style of hunting points made of steel that were very similar to the medieval bodkin points used for warfare by the English archers who had perfected his favorite style of bow. These heavier blades could be re-sharpened over and over again, and most importantly, would easily penetrate bone without breaking. Mitch had no doubt that if he placed the shot correctly, the arrow would penetrate into the man's brain as surely as a bullet, which was his best chance of taking him down.

When he released the string and heard the solid thunk of the arrow strike, he knew he was right. The man fell in his tracks without uttering a syllable, and because the point was likely lodged in the back of his skull, the arrow did not over-penetrate to go flying across the clearing where the others might see or hear it. Mitch breathed a sigh of relief. The six men remaining around the fire were too occupied with their laughing and talking to have heard the sounds of the bowstring, the arrow strike, or the body when it fell. And Mitch knew that hours of looking into the fire would effectively blind them to anything in the dark shadows beyond the circle of light cast by its flames, making it impossible to see movement out here from their perspective.

He was shooting from a low kneeling position, situated beneath the leafy foliage of several small bay trees that would keep him in the darkest shadows and hide the motion of drawing the bow. Before taking out the first man, he had placed several arrows at the ready on the ground in front of him, and next to them, the Remington 870 with a round in the chamber and the safety already off.

Just as he'd expected, when the man he'd shot didn't return to the fire after several minutes, the others began to wonder why. He heard them call his name and heard them ragging the second guy who walked straight to the side of the camper to look for his friend. Mitch waited until he was far enough from the fire that the others couldn't see him but not quite close enough that he would see the body of the fallen one.

When he released his second arrow, the shot was a repeat performance of the first. Like the first man, this one dropped instantly. Mitch readied another arrow immediately, knowing his luck with remaining unheard and unseen was about to run out. When one of the other five men called for the two in the woods and still didn't get an answer from either, he got up with his weapon to come look. Mitch knew that the game was over and the real fight was on.

He drew the bow and took down this third target, not caring that he was still out in the open among his friends, and when the man fell with an arrow through his chest, Mitch reached for the shotgun. The four remaining men never really had chance. The element of surprise was just too complete, and Mitch had eight rounds of double-aught buck shot at his disposal for as fast as he could pull the trigger and at a range from which he really couldn't miss. The only thing he had to worry about was watching his line of fire to avoid shooting into the buildings behind his targets. When one of the men made a desperate attempt to low crawl under the trailer, Mitch hesitated to shoot because it was just too close, but then he heard the crack of April's rifle and saw that he wouldn't have to. The man collapsed to the ground, still moving but not going anywhere until she fired two more shots in rapid succession and then all was still in the clearing except for the dancing flames of the fire.

Mitch reached into his pockets for more shotgun shells and fed them into the magazine by feel. A horrified scream startled him as he was about to step forward, and he saw a woman in a bathrobe with long, wild blonde hair run barefoot out into the clearing by the fire. She screamed again and then fell to the earth beside one of the men and wailed, grabbing him with both hands and shaking him as if to make him get back up. Mitch cautiously emerged from the woods and, keeping the shotgun leveled on the woman. He didn't want to shoot her, though if he saw a weapon, he wouldn't hesitate to do so. But she was so distraught over the dead man, she was not an immediate threat. Mitch kept her covered while he picked up the weapons the fallen men had dropped. There was a bolt-action deer rifle, a lever-action carbine, and, on the ground behind one of the chairs, an AR-15 that he recognized immediately as his dad's patrol rifle. As he bent to pick it up, April walked into the firelight, her carbine also pointed in the general direction of the grieving woman.

"Are you okay?" he asked April, still keeping his voice low.

"I'm fine. I can't believe they never even had a chance to shoot back."

"Yeah, so far, so good. But there could be others inside; she was," he nodded at the woman, then stepped closer to question her.

"I'm looking for my sister. I know these men took her and her friend. Where are they?"

The woman ignored him until Mitch got her attention by pushing the muzzle of his shotgun against the side of her head.

"Inside," she said.

"Is there anyone else in there?"

"No! Everyone is dead! You've killed my husband!"

Mitch turned back to April. "You wait here and keep her covered while I go look for Lisa and Stacy."

Not sure if the woman was telling the truth or not, he stepped into the shadows between the cabin and the mobile home, looking and listening before proceeding around to the front. He knew there was some risk of encountering another armed family member or friend of the seven slain men, but since they had been watching the camp for so long before the attack, he doubted there were any other men around. He couldn't discount the possibility of another woman or a small boy with a gun, though, so he was extremely cautious.

"LISA! STACY! ARE YOU IN THERE? IT'S ME, MITCH!"

There was no reply. He called out their names again and then stepped around to the front of the trailer. The door was shut, but he noticed the door of the cabin was open. He figured the woman must have run out of that one, and he started up the steps, keeping the muzzle of the shotgun pointed ahead of him to clear the way if needed. He was about to call his sister's name when he heard a frightened voice from just beyond the doorway.

"Mitch?"

"LISA!"

His sister's voice was unmistakable. He sprang up the steps and through the open door. The room he entered was a kitchen, with a roughly built table in the middle, on top of which was a burning kerosene lantern. The light from the oil lamp was bright enough to illuminate the whole interior, which was small and quite bare. Along the back wall was a wood stove and some plywood counters with a few pots and pans on them. Adjacent to that wall was one other small room that was connected to the kitchen by an entryway with no door. To close it off from the kitchen and the only exit from the cabin, someone had nailed several pieces of two-by-four and two-by-six lumber across it in a haphazard fashion to form bars. Mitch picked up the lantern and stepped closer, shining its light through the makeshift prison bars, where he saw two frightened but very much alive teenaged girls huddled together on the floor in the far corner.

"LISA! STACY! Are you two okay? Are you hurt?" They looked all right, considering the circumstances, but both of them looked at him with wide eyes. Mitch remembered the wild camouflage patterns April had painted on his face and wiped at it with his sleeve. "Sorry about that. It really *is* me, Lisa."

He glanced back around the kitchen and the doorway he'd come through to make sure he was still alone. There was no one else here but the two girls. The woman wailing outside reminded him April was still out there, and he yelled to her to let her know Lisa and Stacy were here. The he saw an axe leaning against the wall near the woodstove and quickly dashed over and grabbed it.

"You two stay back, Lisa! I'm going to get you out of there. He slung the shotgun over his back to get it out of the way and swung the axe with both hands, quickly hacking through the board barricade until he was able to pull the broken pieces aside and get through. Then he threw the axe down and rushed to crouch in front of Lisa and Stacy, taking them both into his arms and hugging them close.

"I thought you were dead, Mitch," Lisa cried. "I thought you and Momma and Daddy were all dead. Where are they? Are they here, too? I knew Daddy would find those bad guys and make them sorry for what they did if he was still alive."

"It's all right, Lisa. I've been trying to get back to you ever since the lights went out. Momma and Daddy are not with me, but I'm sure they're trying to get here, too. I'm sure it won't be much longer."

"They killed my brother," Stacy said, tears streaming down her face as she pulled away from Mitch's embrace.

"No! He's not dead, either. We found him, Stacy. That's how I knew you two were here. Jason told us what happened. He was hurt bad, but he's going to be okay. We took him back to my house. He's there right now." Mitch saw Stacy's eyes light up, and Lisa was clearly happy to know that Jason was all right. Mitch didn't see any sign that either of them had been hurt, and that was a surprise, considering Jason's condition when he and April found him. "Are you sure you two are all right? Did those men do anything to you?"

"No," Lisa said. "That woman, the one that's screaming so loud, she wouldn't let them. They argued about it. One of them was her husband, and two of them were her brothers. They put us in here so we couldn't get away. I don't think she could have kept them away from us much longer, maybe not even tonight. There was another wife or girlfriend of one of them, too. She was arguing with them about leaving us alone, too, and I saw her get knocked down really hard by the man she was with. I don't know where she is now. She ran away into the woods, I think."

Mitch was surprised that just two women had been able to stop all those men for so long, but then he thought they probably figured they had all the time in the world and that the two women who were protesting would give in eventually. He was glad he hadn't shot the woman outside now that he knew she helped his sister, but he didn't know what was going to become of her now.

Were those seven the only men around? Did they have other friends and relatives that may come here later or may have been here and just gone somewhere temporarily? The one thing he did know was that he had no intention of hanging around to find out.

"Come on. Let's get out of here. Is that old truck still running okay, Lisa?"

"I think so. They've been driving it around and coming and going in it ever since they took it and brought us here in it. I've been hearing it racing up and down the road out there. All they've been doing is drinking and raising hell."

"Well, they're finished now. When we go outside, I want you two to try not to look at the bodies out there, okay? I used Daddy's shotgun and my bow, and it's not pretty and definitely not something you want getting stuck in your memory. I've got a friend out there I want you to meet, though, and I think you're going to really like her."

"You've got a girlfriend?" Lisa asked.

"Not exactly, she . . ." Mitch's answer was cut short by the report of another gunshot from out back. His heart nearly stopped when he heard it, because he instantly knew it was not loud enough to be the sound of April's 5.56mm carbine. It sounded more like the crack of a pistol shot. "Get down and stay where you are!" he ordered the girls, as he swung the shotgun around from his back.

Before he could make it to the door, another shot stopped him momentarily in his tracks. This one *was* a rifle shot, he was sure of that. With his finger on the trigger, ready to blast anything that moved, he stepped outside and descended the steps to the ground. He stopped behind the corner of the building, and called out in a loud whisper, "April? Are you all right?"

For a very long moment, there was silence. Then he heard a strained voice, "Mitch . . . Mitch!"

It was April's voice. He felt a huge relief just knowing she was alive, having feared the worst the instant he heard the shot. But when he rounded the corner and saw her down on her knees, using the carbine like a crutch under one arm and her hand bloody, clutching at the side of her chest, he feared the worst all over again.

He took in the scene before him and instantly knew what had happened: the woman who had been weeping hysterically over the dead man on the ground was now sprawled lifeless on top of him, blood spreading onto her robe from the exit wound in her back. Beside her outstretched hand on the ground was a small stainless steel revolver, the kind designed for deep concealed carry, a weapon of last resort. She had shot April with it and then April had returned fire and killed her before going down herself.

"APRIL!" Mitch was at her side in an instant. Seeing all the blood on the hand she was holding against the side of her rib cage nearly brought him to tears. "April! Where are you hit?" He put his hand over her bloody one, and with his other arm around her shoulders, eased her to the ground on her back, expecting her to fall over at any second.

"I had no idea she was about to do that," April said. "She was completely ignoring me, just hugging that man's body and crying like I've never heard. Then, before I realized what was happening, she suddenly sat up and put her arm out toward me. I didn't even realize she had a gun until she was pulling the trigger. It felt like fire burning through my side, and I realized I'd been shot. She tried to shoot me again, but her pistol just clicked. That's when I shot her. I just did it without thinking."

Seeing her that way, Mitch felt like he was the one who'd been shot, but he knew he had to stay calm and show no fear or his panic would be infectious to April. "I know it hurts, but I've got to see where you're hit," he said steadily.

April moved her hand away from the wound, but with Mitch's mom's black sweatshirt on, he couldn't see anything, other than that the shirt was a bloody mess. He slid it up from her waist to the level of her bra strap and wiped away some of the blood from her rib cage. The wound was right in line with her second lowest rib; he could see where the bullet tore into skin and muscle, seemingly following the bone like the blade of a knife, ripping a narrow gash a few inches long and probably losing little velocity as it continued on. It couldn't have hit any vital organs, but the nasty swath it cut made it bleed like mad, and the rib that deflected it had to be hurting her plenty.

Mitch glanced back over his shoulder at the little revolver on the ground. It was a .22 caliber, like the rifle he normally hunted with. He had seen little .22 caliber, high velocity bullets do all kinds of strange things when they hit an animal. Sometimes they went under the skin and completely changed directions, doing incredible internal damage. April was lucky the bullet hit her rib at an angle that deflected it away from—rather than into—her chest cavity. People underestimated the .22 because it was so small, but Mitch knew better.

"How bad is it?" April asked.

Mitch smiled, feeling just as relieved as he had a moment ago when he had found his sister alive and unharmed. "You're lucky. The bullet just grazed you. It might have cracked a rib, though, I don't know. I do know you're going to be sore for a while."

Satisfied that he was sure of the track of the bullet and that it had not lodged in her body, he held pressure on the wound with the bloody tail of the sweatshirt as he talked to her. "We'll find something to wrap this with for now, and when we get back to the house, I'll make a better bandage. I'm sorry I was so stupid. That man she was crying over must have had that gun on him, somewhere. I should have checked more carefully."

"It's not your fault," April said. "I should have been paying attention. I should have realized what was happening as soon as she raised her arm, and I should have shot her right then."

"It would have surprised anybody. I'm surprised, too, after what Lisa and Stacy just told me. It was this woman and another one that ran away who kept these men from the two of them all this time."

"You found Lisa and Stacy? They're both okay?"

"Yes. Here, let me help you over to the truck, and then I'll go in and bring them out. I want you to meet my sister."

TWENTY-ONE

When the four of them pulled out of the Wallace place, Mitch was driving, Lisa was sitting on the middle of the bench seat beside him, and April was curled up against the passenger's side door, trying to make herself comfortable as she kept pressure on her wound to control the bleeding. Stacy volunteered to ride in the back of the truck to give April more room and help Mitch keep a lookout as they got out of the area as fast as possible.

When they were up to speed on the road, April began to feel like they had actually pulled off their midnight raid and were going to get out of there in one piece—even if that piece was a little worse for the wear. She knew she was lucky, though. If that woman's aim had been better it could have easily meant the end of the journey for her. The pain was bad enough, even if her wound wasn't life threatening. She felt certain her rib was cracked, and the stinging sensation from where the bullet had cut through her flesh had barely abated, despite the two shots of whiskey she'd drank from a bottle Mitch found in the cabin.

Taking part in the ambush of the seven men had been surreal for her, even before the deadly encounter with the grieving woman. She had mercilessly shot a man to death—a man who was trying desperately to crawl for cover—but in doing so she felt nothing. She had been in a state of detachment, acting as the scene unfolded. And when the woman shot her, her decisive reaction was practically automatic. Maybe all that would bother her later, but in reality, she doubted that it would. She certainly had no regrets about killing that man on the road the day she met Mitch, especially after learning of the murdered couple inside the nearby house.

Other than getting shot herself, the biggest surprise for April was that they had succeeded in carrying out their plan and had actually found Mitch's sister and her friend. She had not expected to find them in the condition they were in, if alive at all, after being in the hands of men capable of what they'd done to Jason. Before coming here, she had dreaded what they might find even if they succeeded in taking out the bad guys. It was simply amazing how well Mitch planned and executed that attack, given how little time he had to work with. She knew luck had played a large part in it, too, of course, especially the luck of having them all in one place, out in the open around that campfire. But Mitch's skill with his bow and even the shotgun would impress anyone, and she was glad that she didn't let him down by freezing up or hesitating when he needed her.

As for Stacy and Lisa, they were traumatized, which was completely understandable. But once Mitch explained who April was and why she was there, both girls opened up to her and worried about her wound instead of talking about their own ordeal. Before driving away from the property, Mitch gathered up all the weapons the fallen men had dropped and put them in the back of the truck, except for his father's AR-15, which he put on the seat beside him. He checked the cabin and trailer for more weapons, but found nothing, then set about the grisly task of searching each of the dead men's pockets until he found the one that held the ignition key to the truck. He then looked around the buildings until he found three extra five-gallon jerry cans of gasoline, which he tied down in the back.

"I guess I'm glad they stole these from somewhere. At least we'll have enough to get back to the house and then get the boat to the river."

When Mitch slid behind the wheel and turned the key, the engine turned over and sputtered to life. April felt a flood of relief that made her temporarily forget her pain, but she was reminded of it quickly as the rough-riding antique truck bounced along on the winding country roads leading back to the Henley land. The trip back didn't take long, though, as it was just a few miles by road. When Mitch turned onto the lane and pulled up to the front of the house, he quickly shut off the engine and jumped out of the cab to call out to Jason, letting him know it was them and not one of the Wallace men who had taken the truck.

April could have made it in the house just fine by herself, but Mitch was around to her side and had the door open before she could get out. He had an arm around her as he guided her up the steps and into the house where he led her to the sofa in the den. Stacy went to a closet in the bathroom to get towels, and Lisa went to her mom's bedroom to find April some clean clothes. When they had cleaned up all the blood, April was surprised to see the jagged gash the little .22 caliber bullet had made as it tore a path through the skin at her side.

"It looks worse than it is," Mitch said. "But it's a lot better that it made a gash like that and kept on going, instead of getting lodged inside you. This way at least I don't have to dig it out with my Bowie knife like I've seen them do on all those Western movies."

"Yeah, right. I don't know that digging around with a knife would hurt any worse though. I can't believe how much pain such a shallow wound caused, and with that little .22."

"It's because of the way it scraped along your rib, and it was probably an expanding hollow point bullet. That's why it tore up so much skin. You wouldn't be here if it had gone a couple inches to the right."

"I know. I'm lucky, I guess, just a lot of blood but no permanent damage."

"Let's see if we can get this bleeding stopped for good. You might be sore for a while, and you might have a scar, but I think it will heal just fine."

Mitch used some large gauze pads and tape from the family medicine cabinet to make a bandage over her wound. Aside from the pain, she hadn't realized how exhausted she was until everyone in the house had exchanged their stories of what they'd been through since the power went out. It seemed impossible, listening to Mitch recount their journey, that the last time she had slept was near the bridge over Black Creek just outside Brooklyn, and that was less than twenty-four hours ago! Since then, they had canoed from Brooklyn to here, gathered supplies, prepared the tractor and boat to go to the Leaf River, found Jason, and brought him back to the house. Then they had canoed downriver to sneak up on the Wallace place, killed the men who had kidnapped Lisa and Stacy, and she had gotten shot in the process!

No wonder she was tired! When Mitch suggested they all get some sleep before trying to do anything else, April did not object.

Thanks to her exhaustion, and probably helped by the whiskey, it was close to noon when she finally woke, feeling rested but still in pain. When she checked her bandage she saw that it had not bled through and figured that was a good sign. She wondered what would happen now, with Mitch reunited with his sister and Jason in no condition to do much of anything. She suspected Mitch might not be too keen on carrying on with their plan to go to the Leaf River and Hattiesburg, especially now that she was wounded, too. She certainly hoped he didn't think she intended to stop now.

She went into the kitchen, where he had already made coffee over the camp stove, and after looking at her wound, he assured her that he intended to make good on his promise to help her get back to her Kimberly. "What about Lisa?" April asked. "I don't expect you to leave her after everything that's happened."

"I'm not. She's insisting on going with us, and I've decided I'm okay with that. Even though we have the truck, I still think it's much better to go to Hattiesburg by boat on the Leaf River. I feel pretty good about our chances of getting you there without running into much trouble. The truck will still be handy, though, because that John boat is small enough that we can load it in the back. It will be much faster than towing the boat behind that old tractor. Stacy wants to stay here with Jason, and I think that's best. They will be well-armed, and if things go as well as I hope they will, Lisa and I shouldn't be gone longer than twenty-four hours."

"You could just drop me off at the river with the boat if you want. There's no need for you and Lisa to go to Hattiesburg. I can drive a boat like this. The bleeding has completely stopped. And I know this is where you want to be."

"I want to be wherever you are . . ." Mitch said, before he could stop himself. Immediately he flushed and looked down at his feet to hide it.

April was not surprised to hear this. It was obvious that Mitch had developed quite a crush on her. She knew when they first met that he was attracted to her, and that attraction had grown much stronger as the days went by and they bonded through the dangers they'd experienced. She found herself attracted to him, too, despite the fact that he was younger and still in high school. He was certainly more mature than anyone else his age she'd ever met, and probably more mature than David in many ways, but David was the father of her child.

"I meant I just want to make sure you're going to be okay," Mitch said when he regained his composure. "You've done so much to help me. I can't let you go on alone without knowing if you even get there okay. Lisa and I will be fine. She's tough and can handle the trip, so don't worry about that."

April opened her mouth to say something to Mitch about how she felt, but she knew it would only complicate things. She changed course and asked, "Do we still have to wait until it gets dark again to go up the river?"

She could see that Mitch was relieved that they weren't going to linger on his accidental admission. "No, I don't think it will matter that much. I know you must be incredibly tired of all the delays. I'm going to tell Lisa to get ready, and then we'll get the boat moved from the trailer to the back of the truck so we can get going immediately—if you feel up to it, that is."

"Absolutely! I'm ready to leave as soon as you are."

* * *

An hour later Mitch was once again driving the Ford pickup, with Lisa in the middle between him and April, and the John boat tied in the bed with the bow hanging several feet past the tailgate. The drive to the Leaf River took less than a half hour, but it seemed like just a few minutes to April because as Mitch drove she was busy answering Lisa's questions about her baby and what it was like in New Orleans when the power went out. Like her brother, Lisa was at home out here in the country, but unlike him, she also seemed fascinated with city life and wanted to know all about it.

"Do you think you'll ever be able to go back to New Orleans?" Lisa asked. "Jason says they're never going to get the power on because he thinks the pulse shut it down all over the world. He says things are just going to keep getting worse and just about everybody is going to die except the ones that revert to savages. Do you think he's right?"

"I don't think it's quite *that* bad, but it could be a long time before it gets fixed. I don't think it affected the whole world. Your brother doesn't, either. Do you, Mitch? We were talking about it, and he told me about a documentary he'd seen about solar flares that said if a big one disrupted electrical power grids and did other damage on Earth, it would only affect the side of the planet that was exposed to the sun when it hit."

"So, if that's the case, things could be totally normal in China and other countries on the opposite side?"

"Yeah, I think so. That's hard to imagine considering how it is here, though."

"Do you think those other countries will help us get our lights back on?"

"I would hope so. I'm betting that there are a lot of people working on it right now, at least somewhere."

"Yeah, just not in Mississippi," Lisa said. "We're always last in everything. That's what all my teachers say."

"Sometimes that's a good thing, too," Mitch said.

They came to several intersections and forks in the gravel roads Mitch had picked for the route, and at each new turn, April half expected to encounter someone else in the road, injured like Jason or menacing them with guns like so many others had. But these roads were deserted. The last turn took them down a narrow gravel lane past a sign that said "Boat Ramp" and ended in a loop with a steep, concrete ramp sloping off into the muddy brown waters of a river much wider than Black Creek.

"Here we are," Mitch said, as he parked the truck. "The Leaf River! All we have to do is run it upstream to get to Hattiesburg."

Launching the boat only took a few minutes. With the gear emptied out on the ground, Mitch and Lisa were able to easily carry it down the ramp to the water's edge without April's help and then go back for the equipment and the outboard. Mitch pulled the truck over to one side and parked it out of the way, opening the hood to remove the spark plug wires, which he put in one of the bags they were taking with them.

"Hopefully, it'll still be here when we get back," he said.

April and Lisa got into the boat now reloaded with gear and weapons, while Mitch mounted the old outboard on the transom and connected it via a fuel line to the plastic gas tank. He pulled on the starter several times, getting no response from the engine with the choke in either the on, off, or halfway positions. Nothing seemed to work.

"Probably the spark plug," he said. "I'll try cleaning it." Mitch had a socket to fit the plug in his bag of tools and gear. He removed the plug and April could clearly see it needed cleaning when he showed it to her. Using the smallest blade of his pocketknife, he scraped away the black soot from the contacts and reinstalled the plug. This time, the engine sputtered to life on the third pull. It idled roughly and smoked, but Mitch assured her that was nothing to worry about. When they were all aboard, he pushed the boat away from the bank with a paddle and put the engine in gear.

As bend after bend of lonely woods and sandbars slipped past, April began to hope that at last she was finally going to make it. This would be the last leg of the long and difficult journey. The biggest question in her mind now was whether or not Kimberly and David were going to still be where they were supposed to be.

For the first few miles, they saw nothing but uninhabited forests. To April, they looked every bit as much a wilderness as the officially designated wilderness lands they had traversed on Black Creek. But then they came to a bridge crossing and everything changed. The first bridge was a railroad span, but a half-mile upstream of that, a larger concrete bridge that Mitch said was a state highway arched over the river. The bridge itself was deserted, but Mitch pointed out that wherever there was road access to a river like this, there were usually homes or at least weekend getaway camps. At this particular bridge crossing, there were both, and as they approached, April could see people milling about in the open spaces among the buildings atop the high banks.

"Keep that rifle handy," he told her as he held the throttle steady.

April didn't have to be told. She was nervous, though, even with it across her knees, her finger on the trigger guard. She felt very vulnerable passing so close to all these people. She hoped that the pain from the wound in her side would not inhibit her ability to handle the rifle. Even if it didn't, what if the people on land shot first? She realized the three of them wouldn't have much of a chance out there in the middle of the wide river, passing by not much faster than sitting ducks. She felt the eyes upon her as they motored under the bridge, but no one raised a weapon. Maybe it was because these people were fairly self-sufficient and had what they needed. But it would probably be different if they stopped there, asking for something. Once again, she was glad to be traveling with someone as knowledgeable and well prepared as Mitch. When she thought back on the days since she'd met him, she realized that not once had he needed to ask a stranger for anything.

The only contact they had with anyone from the community on the riverbank was just upstream from the bridge where they had to run parallel to a long sandbar. A group of boys were out there in the open, some fishing and some apparently just playing. Most of them looked to be under twelve years old. They yelled at the sight of the passing boat and gave chase along the water's edge, a couple of them picking up rocks or pieces of driftwood which they hurled at them in an attempt to get them to stop.

"HEY! COME BACK!"

A rock bounced off the side of the aluminum hull and hit the river with a big splash. April heard another one whiz past her head, missing by inches.

"PULL OVER! YOU CAN'T TAKE THAT BOAT UP OUR RIVER!"

Mitch motored on indifferently. April was glad to see that none of these little would-be river pirates had a gun. It might be too tempting for them to pass up a shot with the prospect of taking a boat with a working motor and a supply of gasoline. But that threat was soon forgotten as they were back in isolation with the rounding of one more bend in the river.

"How much farther?" She turned to ask him.

"Not much, maybe ten miles. We should be close in an hour or so."

TWENTY-TWO

Mitch didn't know every bend in the Leaf River the way he knew Black Creek, but he did know which road or highway each of the bridge crossings represented and how many there were between where they'd launched and Hattiesburg. As they got near the outskirts of the small city, he pulled over on a sandbar to study his dad's topographical maps and take another look at an interesting option he'd seen when discussing the location of David's parents' house with April the day before.

By entering the city through the back door, which was essentially what the Leaf River represented, they would have a much better chance of avoiding obstacles like roadblocks and confrontations with other people. The river didn't run through the heart of the city, but it was reasonably close to the downtown area and less than two miles from the neighborhood where David's parents' house was located. An unexpected feature that had caught Mitch's attention when looking at the maps was a small creek that flowed right through that neighborhood. Winding among the city streets, and probably altered and contained by culverts and other flood prevention structures, it made its way through the residential area where the house was located and then through industrial areas downstream, before eventually emptying into the Leaf River on the outskirts of town.

The creek was not big enough to permit travel by boat; that was obvious from its relative size on the map. Even a canoe probably couldn't negotiate more than a short distance of the lower end of it, but that was okay. What interested Mitch was that, whether it could be navigated or not, the creek was a route: a likely unused and mostly unknown route from the river to the neighborhood they needed to reach—and such a route was better than any road.

Mitch was familiar with urban creeks like these—he had explored one just like this on numerous family trips to visit his cousins in Jackson. They had a creek behind their house that was hidden from the yard by a fence and overgrown with cattails and thickets. His aunt and uncle had warned him to stay out of it, because they said it was full of snakes and other dangers, but that hadn't fazed Mitch at all. With his cousins in tow, he had explored it and the stream that ran in it, following it all the way to where it emptied into the swamps of the Pearl River.

Knowing how that little creek was so off the radar of even the people who lived right beside it, Mitch was excited to find one so similar on the map, winding among of the residential areas of Hattiesburg to the Leaf. Just as they had used that small branch of Black Creek to sneak up to the Wallace place in the dark, following such a creek would ensure they would not get lost as long as they kept it in sight.

While they were stopped, he worked out their location on the map and memorized every bend of the river between there and the mouth of the obscure little creek. This would be the last stop, and he had high hopes that they could get there undetected, because the entrance to the creek was just upstream from the municipal sewage treatment facility. There was nothing else in that part of the city but old abandoned industrial areas near the railroad tracks.

"How far will we have to walk?" Lisa asked.

"It looks like it's about a mile and a half. Hard to tell, exactly, with the way that little creek winds. I've gotta warn you, though, it may be as much wading as walking. And the water may be nasty, but it'll be a lot better than getting shot at walking up the street—or having our weapons taken away by cops or something."

"I don't mind wading," Lisa said. "As long as April gets back home to her baby."

Mitch agreed.

"Look," April said. "You've done enough. If you'll just loan me this map and let me take the rifle, you can just drop me off at the mouth of that creek and I can find my way there. There's no sense in the two of you risking that trip into the city. What if someone comes along and finds the boat while you're gone? Then you'd be stuck with no way to get back to your house."

"I won't hear of it," Mitch said. "I'm not about to drop you off and leave without knowing if you ever found Kimberly and David or not. That's not an option, and it wouldn't be even if you were not injured. We'll be fine. With a route like this to get there, I'm not really worried about running into trouble. If we do, then three is better than one."

Twenty minutes after they shoved off again, Mitch spotted the mouth of the small creek flowing into the river from an opening in the bank to their left. There was nothing around the opening but scrubby woods; the only sign they were near a city was the railroad bridge upstream in the distance. Mitch slowed the engine down to idle speed and steered into the entrance. It was just wide enough to go upstream a bit and get the boat out of sight of anyone passing by on the river, but when he pulled up the bank and they got out, he still took the precaution of removing the spark plug from the outboard and hiding the paddle. He considered taking the outboard off and hiding it, then sinking the boat completely in the shallows, but decided against it as they might need to make a quick escape and it would take too long to recover it and get going again. Instead he pulled it into some reeds and tied the boat securely to a nearby tree. The only way anyone would find it would be by walking along the creek bank from the opposite direction or by entering the branch in a boat from the river, as they had. All he could do was try not to worry about it.

When they started walking, he had the shotgun slung over his shoulder and muzzle down by his side, and in his left hand he carried the bow, an arrow nocked and held in position across the riser with his index finger. He instructed Lisa to stay right behind him. She was carrying the .22 hunting rifle. April brought up the rear, walking with the 5.56mm carbine at the ready and the bow and quiver he'd given her out of the way on her back. She seemed to be doing okay and was able to walk at a pace that did not slow them down. He knew she was in pain, though; she just didn't complain about it.

The lower reaches of the creek were like any other stream in the region, the banks overgrown with vegetation and the streambed a mix of dark, smelly mud, red clay, and white sand. Getting through the underbrush required bending and weaving and making detours around briar thickets, and they had not gone far before they had to wade midstream in water almost waist deep when there was no other way around.

But the part of the creek bed still in its natural state was relatively short. They had only gone a few hundred yards upstream when the natural clay and mud banks were replaced by concrete retaining walls installed by the city. Looking less like a stream and more like a man-made ditch, this corridor was still hidden from the outside world by dense thickets of overhanging bushes growing atop the walls on either side. Mitch knew that beyond those walls they were now passing in close proximity to streets and buildings. In normal times they would have heard traffic noises, but this afternoon the only sounds of the city were faraway barking dogs and the occasional distant shout from somewhere among those silenced streets.

Mitch moved slowly, stopping to look and listen often, just as he had when approaching the Wallace place. Lisa already knew the drill from hunting with him, and Mitch knew that April had caught on fast the previous night, so there was no need for any of them to speak. The ditch soon began crossing under city streets as they traveled farther upstream. From studying the map in advance with April, Mitch knew how many to count before they would be in the vicinity of the house they were looking for. In some places the six-foot wooden privacy fences of backyards that were adjacent to the creek were visible from the ditch. Mitch could only hope no one would see their movement through the cracks or from windows of some of the houses that were situated high enough to have a view of the drainage.

The street they were looking for spanned the creek atop a giant concrete culvert. Getting out of the ditch here was not easy. Mitch handed his bow to Lisa and pulled himself up hand-over-hand, and then after she passed all the weapons up to him, he gave them a hand and helped them gain the top of the concrete wall. April grimaced with pain as soon as her full weight was on her arms, but she kept quiet.

When they emerged from the bushes surrounding the ditch and stepped up to the edge of the street, the scene that greeted them was like something from the aftermath of a war. A school bus that must have been on its morning route the day of the pulse was stopped in the middle of the street, its yellow paint blackened from fire as all of the tires had been burned sometime since it came to rest. The house immediately adjacent to it was a burned-out shell, and farther down the street was evidence of more house fires. Those houses that had not been burned had broken windows and bashed-in doors. Mitch slung the bow over his shoulder and put the arrow back in his quiver, deciding the situation warranted carrying his shotgun at the ready instead as they started walking.

Despite the apparent rampage that had taken place here, the neighborhood was eerily quiet now. There was no sign that anyone was in these houses today, and that did not bode well for finding David and Kimberly at David's parents' house, as it was just four blocks away from where they exited the ditch.

"Oh my God," April said. "Where has everybody gone? What happened here?"

"Looters," Mitch said. "Looking for food or whatever they could find, probably. It looks like this happened a couple of days ago, at least."

"We're too late!" April said, with panic in her voice. "Come on, I know where we are now," she said, looking around at the next intersection. "The house is not far."

Mitch gave in to her desire to quicken the pace. He didn't see the need for stealth at this point, as it certainly seemed like the neighborhood had been taken for all it was worth, destroyed, and then abandoned. They passed more stalled cars with smashed-in windows, and more burnt houses, some of them still smoldering and smoking. Then after one more block, April sprinted ahead, crossing a green lawn to a house with brown cedar siding and a two-car garage facing the street.

"Wait, April! Be careful!" Mitch and Lisa caught up with her as she vaulted up the steps to the front porch. The house had not been set afire, but the front door had been smashed in and was hanging ajar. April couldn't wait any longer and went in, her carbine at hip level and at the ready. When Mitch followed her into the foyer he could see that the house had been ransacked like the others on the street. Drawers and cabinets were open and random stuff was strewn everywhere. But it was clear that there was no one here now, at least not anyone alive.

Just enough fading afternoon light filtered through the windows to allow them to find their way around inside. April went straight for the bedroom where David and Kimberly slept when they visited his parents. Mitch was right behind her as she made her way to the empty baby bed and collapsed beside it, reaching through the rails to clutch the blanket that certainly still smelled of Kimberly. He didn't know what to say as she pulled the blanket through the bars and buried her face into it sobbing, but when he glanced back into the bed where the blanket had been, something caught his eye.

"April! There's a note! Look!"

Mitch reached into the bed and got it for her. Of course, if David was going to leave her a note this is where he would put it, because he would know that if she somehow made her way here, this was the first place she would look. Mitch and Lisa could not refrain from looking over her shoulder as she read the note.

April was on her feet again immediately, transformed from utter hopelessness and despair to radiant joy. David's message was a short one: He and Kimberly had gone with his parents to take shelter in the nearby church that his mother and father belonged to. Members were gathering there with all the supplies and weapons they could bring from their homes to protect themselves from the gangs that were taking over the city. April knew right where the church was, as she had been there with David and his parents once to attend his cousin's wedding.

"Look at the date he put on there, April. That was what, five days ago? That means they probably took shelter there before all this looting happened."

"Yeah, I know it! Let's go. We can get there before dark if we hurry." She was stuffing the blanket in her small pack as she spoke, not about to leave it behind.

Her sense of relief and renewed hope was contagious, and Mitch and Lisa were just as eager as she was to get to that church and see her reunited with her child. When April turned and led the way back through the house to the front door, Mitch didn't try to stop her, because he was sure no one had seen them enter. But when she reached the threshold, something shattered one of the windows on the opposite side of the kitchen, beyond the foyer. Only a fraction of a second later a rifle report echoed from across the street out front. Mitch barely had time to register how wrong he'd been.

"GET DOWN, APRIL!" he screamed, as he grabbed Lisa and pulled her to the floor with him.

April didn't have to be told twice. She dove back into the kitchen and took cover behind the refrigerator as several more shots rang out and bullets tore through sheetrock and splintered wood door casings. The firing sounded like it was coming from more than one weapon, but it was not the rapid fire of semiautomatic rifles. Ordering Lisa to stay put, Mitch belly-crawled to the front living room where he raised his head just high enough to get a quick look outside.

He saw two runners dash out from behind a parked car across the street, while another person remained in position, still firing a steady barrage of shots to provide cover for the two who were trying to get closer. Even at a glance, Mitch could tell that the two who were running were young teens. They were probably a gang of looters, maybe part of the same bunch that had already ransacked the house before. They were both carrying rifles, and they had split up to try and get to flank positions on either side of the house.

Mitch jabbed the muzzle of his shotgun through the closest windowpane to open fire, but the nearest runner dropped out of sight in the drainage culvert in front of the house before he could take aim and the other one made it to the corner of the adjacent house on the same side of the street. The shooter behind the car was still sending rounds in the vicinity of the front door, where April had almost been hit. Mitch fired a couple of rounds at the car, but he knew the distance was a bit far for buckshot. Cursing under his breath, he withdrew to the hallway to get away from the front wall.

This was serious, and Mitch was thinking fast, trying to come up with a solution. If they went anywhere near the front walls, the only place where they could effectively return fire, it would only be a matter of time before one of them was hit by the high-powered rifle rounds. If the two runners got them pinned down from both sides, there would be no escape. Motioning for Lisa to follow him, he crawled to the kitchen where April was and quickly explained the situation to her.

"I've got to get out the back door and get around to one side somehow. They're trying to surround the house. I don't know how many there are, but I've seen at least three. I need you to trade weapons with me. Take the shotgun and just keep shooting often enough to keep them from rushing the front door. Lisa, you help her out with your .22. Both of you just shoot out toward the street, but stay back here and don't get near the front walls. They may think the shotgun and that .22 are the only weapons we have. I need the carbine for the reach, especially for that guy across the street. Just keep up the noise and try to keep their attention focused on the house."

April took the shotgun and the pile of shells Mitch emptied out of his pockets. "Be careful, Mitch!"

With the Ruger carbine and the one extra thirty-round magazine, he crawled to the sliding glass door off the den that opened onto a patio. After a quick check that no one was in the backyard, he made his exit. Although the house was of wood frame construction with cedar siding, Mitch was glad to see that the raised foundation it was built on was brick-veneer up to a height of about two and a half feet. It would provide reasonable cover as long as he stayed low. He made his way to the back corner and looked out. From this vantage point, he couldn't see the car the most distant shooter was hiding behind, but he was in a position to see the ditch that one of the other two had leapt into. Mitch watched as that kid stuck his head up just enough to fire into the house. Only an inch or so of his skull was visible. The crack of Lisa's .22 and the blast of his shotgun answered the rifle shots coming into the house, echoing out across the once quiet suburban neighborhood, and Mitch knew that all the attackers were still focused on those inside. They thought they had everyone inside pinned down, and had no way of knowing one of their targets was stalking them.

He crawled low and slow along the side of the foundation, sliding through a muddy flowerbed until he reached the front corner of the house. From there, he was only thirty yards or so from both the street and the culvert, and less than a hundred yards from the car at the other house. The one in the ditch was staying low, so Mitch decided to focus on the shooter behind the car. He braced the carbine against his shoulder from the prone position and waited until the rifle barrel appeared over the hood again. When it did, he could only see the top half of the shooter's head. It was a small target with the rough open sights of the Ruger, but Mitch had been hunting with open sights since he'd started out with BB guns. He exhaled slowly and squeezed the trigger. One minute there had been a target, then there was none. He was sure of a hit, even though he couldn't see the fallen body behind the car.

With the rifle from across the street silenced, Mitch

turned his attention back to the kid in the culvert. All the shooting had stopped at this point, and Mitch guessed that the two runners had been depending on the covering fire and didn't know what to do. Hopefully they also didn't know where the rifle shot that had taken out their partner had come from. He was aiming at the approximate point where he had last seen the nearest attacker's head, and suddenly a figure sprang out of the ditch at a dead run in the opposite direction, heading back across the street. Mitch aimed at the center of his back, his finger tightening on the trigger, but he hesitated. He saw the other one running away as well, crossing the street farther up the block. He could have easily taken them both out before they disappeared into the backyards beyond the row of houses across the street, but he couldn't bring himself to shoot them in the back. It was clear that they were just kids, probably no older than Lisa. With the main shooter down, the fight had been taken out of them. He yelled into the house to warn April and Lisa to stay alert and cover him, then worked his way across the street to confirm that the one he'd shot was indeed dead.

"Let's get out of here," he said, as he returned to get April and Lisa.

"Did you hit the one behind the car?" April asked.

"Yes. There wasn't much left of his . . . face," Mitch sputtered, "but he looked a good bit older than those other two boys. Probably some thug they looked up to even before all this happened, and he put them up to it. Letting them take the risk while he stayed back at a distance, thinking he was safe."

"You're not worried they'll try and follow us?"

"No. Those two were scared as hell. I think they've seen the light, and I'll bet that's the last time they'll try to assault an occupied house. I could have killed them easily, but I've about had enough of killing for a while."

"You and me both," April agreed. "I just want to get to that church as fast as possible."

"There might still be some looters out there, even if these kids have run off for good," said Lisa.

"She's right," April said. "All I want to do is run, but it's probably safer to take our time, huh?"

Mitch could see the agony on April's face. "Well, if my years of hunting have taught me anything, it's that a fast moving target is harder to hit than slow one. And even though those kids were probably just following that one guy, they may have retreated just to get some backup. If you're up for it, April, I think we better make a run for it now before anything else happens."

"I think you're right," April said and smiled.

She was so excited about the prospect of seeing Kimberly that she seemed to have forgotten all about her wound. There was no slowing her down, and Mitch and Lisa had a tough time even keeping up. The route to the church took them across Hardy Street, a major thoroughfare through Hattiesburg. Once they were on the other side of the four-lane road, the church was just a couple of blocks away.

Mitch saw that it was an old building, and like many older Protestant churches in the area, the architecture resembled a medieval fortress, with decorative parapets atop the two-story walls and massive double doors of heavy timber guarding the front entrance. The members had added additional fortifications by pushing dozens of vehicles together to form a barricade across the front and sides. Mitch saw from a block away that there were two armed men standing behind the row of big SUVs in front of the doors. Their weapons were AR-15–type rifles, and upon seeing the three strangers running their way, they immediately brought them to ready position.

April, Lisa, and Mitch skidded to a full stop, holding their arms high with their weapons pointing harmlessly to the sky.

"Don't come any closer or we'll shoot!" one of the men shouted. "Just turn around, and go back the way you came!"

"My baby is in there!" April screamed. "I'm here to see her and her father, David Greene. His parents are Mr. and Mrs. Richard Greene. They are members of your church, and I know they are here!"

At this, Mitch could see the men with the rifles discussing something among themselves. They were understandably cautious, considering what had happened in the city.

"You! If you're the mother, leave your weapon and walk slowly up here to the sidewalk. You other two, put your weapons on the ground and keep your hands up where we can see them!"

"It's okay," Mitch said as they all stooped to lay their guns down. "Just do it. We'll be right here. Just walk slowly, like he said. They're pretty nervous. They must have already had a lot of trouble."

Mitch and Lisa could do nothing but watch and wait. They saw April walk up to the row of vehicles, where she was apparently told to stop and keep her hands up, while one of the guards disappeared around the corner. The name Greene definitely registered with these guys, or else they wouldn't have let her get this far. But the minutes dragged by and nothing happened. Mitch was starting to get anxious for April when all of a sudden one of the big front doors swung inward and a small crowd of people rushed out. At the forefront was a slim young man with dark hair, and in his arms was a little girl. April ran forward with unbridled joy and took them both in her arms.

Mitch felt a lump rising in his throat as he realized his journey with her had come to an end. He could no longer ignore what she had said about having a family of her own or pretend it might not be real. April was indeed the mother of a beautiful baby girl, and there in front of him was the father, the three of them locked in an embrace that seemed to never end. Mitch and Lisa picked up their weapons along with April's carbine and bow, and slinging them over their shoulders, walked the rest of the way to the edge of the church grounds, where they stood quietly to one side to await introductions.

THE END

About the Author

SCOTT B. WILLIAMS has been exploring wild places and seeking adventure on both land and sea for most of his life. At the age of twenty-five, he embarked on an open-ended solo sea kayaking journey from his home in Mississippi to the islands of the Caribbean. His nonfiction book *On Island Time: Kayaking the Caribbean* is a narrative of that life-changing journey. His pursuit of adventure travel led him to further develop his wilderness survival skills that began with hunting and fishing while growing up in rural Mississippi. After his Caribbean kayak trip, he spent years testing his skills in a variety of environments throughout North America, using both modern and primitive methods, and traveling both on foot and by canoe and kayak. His enthusiasm for travel by water fueled an interest in a variety of boats and led him to learn the craft of wooden boatbuilding. In addition to building boats, paddling small craft, and offshore sailing, he enjoys backpacking, bicycling, martial arts training, dual-sport motorcycling, and photography. He maintains several blogs related to these pursuits and occasionally writes for magazines, including *Sea Kayaker* and *SAIL*. His most popular blog is *Bug Out Survival* (www.bugoutsurvival.com), which expands on his books *Bug Out: The Complete Plan for Escaping a Catastrophic Disaster Before It's Too Late* and *Bug Out Vehicles and Shelters*. His first work of fiction, *The Pulse: A Novel of Surviving the Collapse of the Grid*, was published in 2012. More information about Scott can be found on his main website, www.scottbwilliams.com. He lives in Prentiss, Mississippi.